F
MUR

Murrow, Liza Ketchum

Twelve days in
  August

2o756

$14.95

| DATE | | | |
|---|---|---|---|
|  |  |  |  |
|  |  |  |  |
|  |  |  |  |
|  |  |  |  |
|  |  |  |  |
|  |  |  |  |
|  |  |  |  |
|  |  |  |  |
|  |  |  |  |
|  |  |  |  |
|  |  |  |  |
|  |  |  |  |

# TWELVE DAYS
# IN AUGUST

# Also by Liza Ketchum Murrow

**FOR YOUNG ADULTS**

*West Against the Wind*
*Fire in the Heart*

**FOR AGES 8–12**

*Dancing on the Table*
*The Ghost of Lost Island*
*Allergic to My Family*

**PICTURE BOOKS**

*Good-bye, Sammy*

# TWELVE DAYS IN AUGUST

*Liza Ketchum Murrow*

*Holiday House/New York*

Library of Congress Cataloging-in-Publication Data
Murrow, Liza Ketchum, 1946–
Twelve days in August : a novel / Liza Ketchum Murrow.
p.    cm.
Summary: Twelve days in August change a sixteen-year-old soccer
player's perceptions of himself, his family, girls, and gays.
ISBN 0-8234-1012-9
[1. Soccer—Fiction.   2. Homosexuality—Fiction.]   I. Title.
II. Title: 12 days in August.
PZ7.M96713Tw      1993      92-54489      CIP      AC
[Fic]—dc20

*For Michael, with love and thanks*

# TWELVE DAYS
# IN AUGUST

# Chapter One

"Why does the first day of practice have to come so soon?" I asked myself, nudging the accelerator. My stepmother's old yellow Subaru rattled on the curves; I was driving a little too fast down the hill, but I didn't want to be late. Crawford, the soccer coach, was nuts about his players showing up on time, and I was finally a junior, ready to try out for varsity, so I couldn't mess up now. I'd been waiting for this day ever since I was six years old and someone showed me how to kick a beat-up ball across our school's rocky playground.

I did a mental check. Cleats oiled and ready; shin guards clean, for once; water bottle full. I'd even brought my best stitched ball. It rolled around in back when I stopped at the light just before the high school. I pulled into the lot, parked at the back, and lugged my stuff out to the field. I was starting to work up a sweat, even though it was still cold and misty down in the valley. Crawford was famous for starting his practices early—too early, if you ask me.

I waved to Craig Duffey, who was J.V. co-captain with me last year. He bounced up and down on his toes, his arms spiraling to warm up. "Hey, O'Connor," he called, "how's it going?"

"Good," I said, which wasn't completely true. I was psyched, but nervous. What if I screwed up royally on the first day? "How about you?" I asked.

He shrugged. "I feel worked up, to tell the truth. Especially this year."

I grinned, relieved to know he felt the same way. "Yeah—me too. It's a dog, isn't it? Last night I dreamed I didn't make the team."

Craig laughed. "Come on, Todd, after subbing in those varsity games last year? You'll be a starter, for sure."

I ducked my head so he couldn't see my red face. Of course I was hoping to start, but I didn't want to get jinxed by sounding too full of myself. "Hope so. *You'll* start, no problem. After all, the best sweeper graduated."

"Yeah, that's an asset. I'm glad I stuck with defense. But there are still some good seniors playing back there. We'll have to wait and see."

We went out on the field and made lazy passes with my ball while more guys straggled over to the bench from the lot. The wet grass soaked through my shoes in no time, but it felt good, warming up, hearing the gentle chunk of leather against our insteps and toes.

"What position you hoping to play?" Craig stopped the ball with his knees and then kicked it across to me.

I shrugged. "Depends where the coach puts Tovitch."

Randy Tovitch, the varsity team's lead scorer last year, usually played striker, my favorite spot on J.V., so I was secretly hoping for left wing, another nice scoring position. And good for someone left-footed, like me.

"Yeah. Randy can play wherever he wants." Craig frowned and rubbed his hand over the short nap of his hair.

"We could too, if we'd scored that many goals," I said.

"Maybe. Crawford's been grooming Tovitch ever since he was a kid—even made it easy on him in algebra last year so he'd have a passing grade." Craig started to say something else, then his face smoothed over. "Here comes the man himself." He nodded toward the parking lot. A bunch of guys from last year's team—seniors now, like Randy—piled out of Tovitch's blue pickup: Dex, Randy's shadow; Rich, a burly kid who played stopper; and Benji, a midfield player. The door slammed; then we heard Randy's hoarse voice. From the way the guys laughed, he must have told a dirty joke. Randy had on an old wool jacket and a stained cap; he looked like he'd just stepped off his dad's log truck. "I hope Crawford doesn't go nuts and make Tovitch captain," Craig muttered.

"He won't," I said, but I wondered. I took the ball down the field and passed it across to Craig. Neither one of us said it, but we were probably thinking the same thing—Randy could play soccer, but he was unpredictable in other ways. I'd learned that my first day of kindergarten, on the early-morning bus ride. Randy, just a year older, was already a legend. When he climbed onto the bus at his stop and swaggered down the aisle, knocking off hats and glowering at us from under his heavy black hair, every kid who had smarts edged toward the windows or looked the other way.

"What about it?" Craig asked as we watched Randy jog across the field. "Think we can handle him?"

"Sure," I said. "After all, it's his game too."

As if he'd heard me, Tovitch stripped off his sweats, grabbed a ball from the coach's bag, and started juggling, wearing a big grin on his face like it was the beginning of summer vacation instead of the end. "He shouldn't be a problem," I said, waving to him.

To my surprise, Randy waved back. "See?" I told Craig. "No problem at all."

Which shows how little I knew about anything.

We didn't have time to think about Randy after that, because the coach arrived on the field with his clipboard under his arm, wearing a tight smile. He rounded us up and gave us a pep talk, then asked the freshmen to introduce themselves. They looked terrified, and I remembered how scared I felt, two years ago, playing with guys twice as big as I was—and too full of themselves.

"All right, listen up," Crawford said. "Get out there and stretch. Exactly twelve days until our first game. Everyone practices together this week. Friday, I make the cuts with the J.V. coach. Sophomores, remember another year on J.V. is an advantage—you play all the time, which means you're an asset at the varsity level."

"Poor suckers, he gives them that same line every year."

I turned around. Randy Tovitch had plunked himself next to me. I gave him a quick smile, then turned back to Crawford. Our coach was in his late twenties and built like me: short and stocky. He was always in training for some marathon or triathlon, so he was strong and fast. Unfortunately, he expected the rest of us to be just as fit, which was impossible. Even though I'd hauled boards around the lumber yard all summer, I knew these first few days would be painful.

As soon as we'd loosened up, Crawford called, "Okay, run down the hill to the river and back. Last one up is ball boy at the end of the morning."

No one wants to collect thirty balls and stuff them into the coach's net bag when you're so tired you can hardly move, so Craig and I bolted across the field, trying to keep ahead of the pack. "Hustle!" Crawford yelled, running alongside. Then he dropped back to encourage the freshmen.

"We'll be so beat . . . after the run . . . Never make it across the field," Craig said, panting, when we started back up the hill. "Painful."

"Always is," I said, but actually I was up for it, in spite of the torture.

When we dragged back to the bench, Crawford tossed us each a ball. "Dribble it up and down the field a few times," he said. "Let me see your footwork."

"Brutal," Craig groaned when the coach set us up to take shots on goal, but he grinned through his sweat just the same—another soccer nut.

After drills were over, Crawford divided us up for a scrimmage. "O'Connor, take left wing," he said. I jogged right out there, not even trying to hide the grin on my face. Was Crawford hearing my prayers, or what? A few juniors sank down on the bench; the same ones who'd warmed it last season. It hurt to look at them.

Randy trotted past me and glanced their way. "Why don't those guys give up now, before it gets humiliating?" he said.

I shrugged. "At least they try."

Randy curled his lip, showing his chipped front tooth; someone had clipped his mouth in a game last year. "Come on, admit you'd rather be out on the field, scoring goals."

"Of course," I said, grinning back. Maybe Tovitch would be all right after all.

Crawford blew the whistle, and we started to play. I felt rusty at first, but pretty soon my feet remembered what to do. It felt great to trap the ball and maneuver it past some defender, then shoot across to the striker. Crawford paced up and down the lines, yelling comments at everyone. "Todd, use both feet! Tovitch, take it on the chest! Dexter, aim the ball! You can do better than that!" And to all of us: "Don't bunch up! This isn't elementary school!"

He made me remember my first team, where the ball was a magnet, sucking every little kid toward it; we'd be scrambling for it all together, leaving the rest of the field empty. I tried to spread out now, moving into the open spots; once Crawford even praised me, calling, "Nice, Todd—now pass; get rid of it!"

After a while, he rotated me out, along with Tovitch and a bunch of last year's starters.

"Aw, come off it, Coach, we just went in," Randy complained.

"Everyone gets a chance, at the beginning," Crawford told him. "Would I have noticed you, sophomore year, if I hadn't played you that first week?"

There wasn't much Tovitch could say to that. Two years ago he was the only sophomore moved up to varsity, so this was his third year on the team. Tovitch went for water, and the coach nodded at me. "Way to hustle, Todd. You've got the power for midfield, too; we'll try you there next time."

I couldn't help smiling, even though I secretly hoped he'd keep me on the front line. Still, I was pleased; Crawford wasn't known for compliments.

I drank a few cups of water, poured some over my head, and flopped onto the bench, groaning. Tovitch sat down beside me. "God, I'm wasted," he complained, stretching.

"Yeah," I said. "My calves will set up like concrete by morning. Hey, look at Drew; he's even faster than last season." Drew Watson was a sophomore; a small compact guy whose legs moved like pistons. He charged straight for the goal and took a shot that almost went in; Ozzie, our goalie, barely saved it.

"Nice one!" Randy called. "Yeah, Drew will play varsity for sure; he's a great wing."

Crawford blew a whistle to stop the play and went out on the field to talk to the guys about something. I couldn't hear what he said, but his hands chopped the air as if he'd found a punching bag.

"Hey, check this out." Tovitch tapped my shoulder and nodded toward the high school. I turned around. Two kids were coming across the parking lot, a boy and a girl. Randy whistled low, under his breath. "Who the hell is *that*?"

He meant the girl, of course. We'd never seen her before, and Griswold Central High was small enough so you knew everybody—especially a girl like this one. She was tall and amazingly thin, with long silvery-blond hair that actually swished when she walked. She looked like the guy beside her; they both had the same pale hair and a funny, light way of moving, as if the grass were spongy. I suddenly realized I was gawking and turned around quickly, but not before the girl noticed and gave me a dazzling smile. She came over and stood in front of us, a brand-new soccer ball tucked under her arm.

"Hi," she said, looking right at me; for someone new, she sure wasn't shy. "I'm Rita Beekman. This is my brother, Alex. Do you know where the girls are practicing?"

My face was getting red; there was nothing I could do about it. Hopefully, I was sweaty enough so she'd think I was hot. "Over there, on the back side of the school," I said, pointing. And then, I guess because she was so pretty, I stood up, even though it made me realize I was at least an inch shorter than she was.

"Are you looking for girls' varsity?" I asked.

She nodded. "We're both juniors. I hope I can make the team. I'm not a star, like Alex." Her brother gave her this pained look. Both juniors—were they twins? Their eyes sure looked identical: an intense, almost navy blue behind pale lashes. I glanced away. I felt like a pig next to this freshly scrubbed girl.

"What's your name?" she asked.

"Todd O'Connor," I said. "And this is Randy Tovitch," I added, because I could feel him giving my back the hairy eyeball.

"Nice to meet you," she said. Then she looked at her brother, Alex, and something weird happened. She didn't say a word, but he acted as if she had; he nodded and said, "Fine—I'll see you later"—and she left.

The guy called Alex glanced at me, then swallowed so hard, his Adam's apple bobbed up and down. I felt sorry for him. I'd hate to change schools now, even though Griswold Central High drives me nuts sometimes. I've lived with my friends' little habits and phobias since kindergarten. Maybe it was time the place got some new blood.

"We just moved to town," Alex said, tossing his hair. "Where's the coach?"

Tovitch pointed down the field. "Right over there, in the green sweat suit. Mr. Crawford, but you can forget the 'mister'; we all do." Tovitch stood up and stuck his chin out toward the new kid, so close Alex took a step back and almost lost his balance. "So, what position do you play?" he asked. Randy's chipped tooth flashed in the sun.

"Left wing," Alex answered, blinking fast. "Or striker." He gave us a tiny wave and walked down the line to Crawford.

"*Left wing,*" Randy whispered in a prissy way. "*Striker.*" He raised one eyebrow, let his wrist dangle, and grinned at me. "What do you think?" he whispered. "A lightweight—or what?"

I shrugged. "Who knows?" Actually, Alex didn't look

like a soccer player. He was tall and almost too thin, and he had this timid, polite look. It was hard to imagine him hustling past a hefty defensive man.

Alex stood quietly near the coach until he got his attention. They shook hands. I couldn't hear what they were saying, but Crawford was obviously peppering Alex with questions from the side of his mouth, although his hawk eyes never left the game. All of a sudden Alex said something that made the coach crane his head up to stare at him—the new guy really was tall—then Crawford grinned, clapped him on the shoulder, blew the whistle, and sent Alex in to play left wing.

"Uh-oh," I said. Randy and I moved closer to the field. It took Alex only about thirty seconds to get hold of the ball; he chest-dropped a high pass, let the ball roll down his thighs, and dribbled out to the side. Our jaws dropped. The kid moved like a dancer; his feet were so fast, he slipped right by two defensive players, keeping hold of the ball as if it were glued to him.

"Pass to the center!" Drew yelled. But Alex had found a hole in the defensive line; he made a beautiful crossing pass, just missing the sweeper. The ball sailed into the far corner of the net, leaving Ozzie face down in the dirt. Alex spun around and jogged easily back up the field, twisting something on his right hand.

Randy's black eyebrows drew close together. "Did you see that? Less than two minutes on the field, and he scores. He's left-footed—and fast." Tovitch inched close to me. "Listen, we'd better be careful. Crawford wouldn't dare move me from striker—but that could be your position Alex just snagged. Who the hell is this guy, anyway?"

"I don't know." I wandered over near Crawford so he'd remember I was there. Even though Randy's attitude was really annoying, he was probably right; as lead scorer last year, he could play where he wanted. But I'd have to hustle—and show this new guy what the deal was. You don't just move into town and shove your way into the forward line the first day of practice. At least, that's what I thought at the time.

# Chapter Two

Everyone was dead by the end of practice—except the new kid. While most of us collapsed on the grass or stood by the cooler, guzzling water, Alex sat with his legs crossed, Indian style; it was years since I'd been able to do that—my leg muscles weren't that flexible. The guy didn't look sweaty or tired, but he still seemed nervous; he kept twisting a ring on his right hand, spinning it around and around like he wasn't used to wearing it—or maybe he just felt like holding on to something.

"All right, pretty good for our first day," Crawford said, pacing up and down. "But we've got work to do. A little tired?" He nudged me with his toe. I groaned.

"Good." Crawford rubbed his hands together. "That means you're hustling."

Craig raised his eyebrows. "How obnoxious. What's with all the enthusiasm?" he whispered.

I shrugged. "Just trying to pump us up."

"Good luck. My body feels like it got run over by one

of those big-mother trucks Randy's dad drives," Craig muttered.

"Listen up," Crawford was saying. "Be here at eight thirty tomorrow. No excuse for skipping or being late. If you want to be on the team, get here on time." He pointed to the new kid, alone at the edge of the circle. "This is Alex Beekman. He's from California, which means he's used to playing soccer year round. He was leading scorer on his team last year, as a varsity sophomore."

Heads were really turning now; a couple of guys whistled. Alex looked down at the ground.

"We're lucky to have him with us," Crawford said. "Introduce yourselves in the next few days, so he knows who's who."

Leading scorer as a *sophomore*? I sighed, pulling off my shin guards. That meant Alex could have any position he asked for.

Tovitch sidled over and elbowed me. "Will you look at that? His ears are bright red," he whispered.

Tovitch was right, Alex's ears and neck were pink. "So?" I said.

"The guy blushes like a girl."

I picked at the grass. I was pretty good at blushing myself; my sister, Molly, loved to tease me when my cheeks matched my hair. Craig glared at Tovitch, then stood up and went over to shake Alex's hand, introducing himself. As the only black guy on the team, maybe Craig knew how it felt to be different. I should have said something to Alex, but for some reason I couldn't move. I just sat there, untying my cleats, while Tovitch made his snide remarks.

"What'd I tell you?" Tovitch hissed. "His *sister* has to drop him off and pick him up. Wimp."

Sure enough, Rita was coming toward us across the field with a couple of girls from the varsity. As soon as Alex saw her, he stood up and waved. Rita had certainly picked the right girls to latch on to: Jen and Trish were popular juniors who loved to flirt with the guys. When they reached the bleachers, Benji and Rich, the two seniors who played defense, started ribbing them. Pretty soon Rita was getting introduced all around. She beckoned to Alex. Instead of ignoring her, the way I would if *my* sister tried to introduce me to her friends, Alex hurried over to his twin like a puppy, tossing his head to flick the hair out of his eyes.

I shoved my ball into the bag. The twins were both going to do all right with the girls, I could see that already. I felt a little jealous, watching Rita smile at everyone. She was like Alex: cool and clean in spite of her workout. Her hair was in a braid now. It looked silky and soft, dangling over one shoulder.

I turned away. You *have* a girlfriend, remember? I reminded myself. At least until Labor Day, when Kai would go home to Boston. Anyway, I wasn't Rita's type. She was the kind of girl who wouldn't notice someone shorter than she was, a guy covered with freckles, his red hair tangled every which way.

Tovitch wandered past, his cleats slung over his shoulder. "Going to the lake?" he asked.

I stared at him, surprised. What was with Randy's new friendliness? "Not today. Blair needs the car."

He shrugged and spoke low, into my ear. "Too bad. We've got some good stuff."

It took me a minute to get it. He was going to smoke dope on the first day of practice? "Hey, didn't you sign the pledge?"

He snorted. "Give me a break, Mister Clean Jeans. A little toke now and then won't hurt anyone, especially *after* practice. You know I'd never be stoned for a game."

I wondered. Last year I'd heard stories about a few seniors dropping acid before a tournament. Tovitch pinched my arm. "Watch out for lover boy," he whispered, and sauntered off to his truck.

*Lover boy?* I shook my head. What was he talking about? Rich, Dexter, and a couple of J.V. players were already sitting in the back of the pickup, jostling each other. When Tovitch reached them, he said something that made them whistle and jeer. I was relieved when his truck squealed out of the lot, scattering stones.

"Excuse me—Todd?" I turned around; Rita and Alex were right behind me.

"Hey," I said to Rita. "How was your practice?"

She smiled. "Fine. The coach is nice—she lets everyone play. I probably won't start—I'm not as fast as Alex—"

"You don't need to be that fast, to play defense," Alex said quickly. His face got hot, and she nudged him.

"Lighten up, bro'," she told him, and then she said to me, "Alex and I always stand up for each other. I guess that's part of being twins. Anyway, I don't care if I play first string, long as I make the team."

"You will," Alex said.

Rita looked at me. "Alex is good, isn't he?" she asked.

"Rita, cool it," Alex protested. His ears were red again.

"Why should I? It's true." She cocked her head to one side, waiting for me to answer.

"Yeah," I said quickly. "He is—I mean, yeah, you are, Alex." I felt like I had marbles in my mouth.

We were near my car; Rita glanced at Alex. "Got any change?" she asked him. "We should call home."

I took a deep breath. "Where do you live? I could give you a ride."

Rita laughed. "In the middle of nowhere; some road called Soldier's Hill. That's okay, our mom said she'd pick us up."

*The middle of nowhere?* Thanks a lot, I thought, but of course I didn't say it out loud. "Soldier's Hill is just off my road," I told her. "I can take you home. Throw your stuff in here."

Rita glanced at Alex, and he nodded. That was the second time I'd seen them do that: talk without saying anything. Man, I'd be upset if my sister Molly could read my mind that way.

I opened the hatch and we tossed water bottles, cleats, and balls into the car. Alex climbed in back and Rita got in front, buckling her seat belt and adjusting it as if she rode in the Subaru every day. Ozzie, our goalie, went past the car, noticed Rita, and whistled. Rita didn't even blink. I ducked my head, feeling hot.

"Better open the windows," I said. "It's pretty rank in here." I jammed a tape into the slot and jacked up the sound; with the wind rushing past, it was hard to hear, which was fine with me. I didn't know what to say to Rita anyway.

"What's the group?" she asked.

"Phish," I said. "The tape's pirated. They started in Vermont; now they're getting big everywhere."

I thought she'd be impressed, but instead she said, "Mind if I turn it down a little?"

"Okay," I said. So the girl had no taste in music. Everything else about her seemed all right. I drove fast past Kai's house, hoping she wouldn't see me go by with a beautiful stranger in the front seat. I was saved; her yard was empty.

"Have you lived here a long time?" Rita asked.

"Almost seventeen years," I said. "Since I was born."

"That must be nice," she said. "My parents like to move around. This is our fifth school. Luckily, we have each other." She said it like it was no big deal, but I wouldn't like that. And I'd certainly never rely on my sister for friendship.

I watched the road; the washboards on the hills were pretty bad and dust billowed up behind us. The Subaru rattled and shook. "Sorry about the car," I said. "It's old and sick, but Blair, my stepmother, refuses to buy a new one. I'm saving up for a car of my own; I've got a long way to go."

Rita watched me, as if she were memorizing my face. Had I said something weird? "Are your parents divorced?" she asked suddenly.

"Rita!" Alex groaned from the backseat, and I twitched, surprised. I'd forgotten he was there.

"Sorry," Rita said. "That's none of my business, is it?"

"It's okay," I said, although, to tell the truth, it wasn't my favorite topic. "My mother died a long time ago. Blair's like my real mother; she's been around since I was small."

Rita was quiet for a minute. She crossed her legs, and I couldn't help noticing how tan and smooth they were, all the way up to her shorts. She turned toward the backseat, and for a second, when I looked in the rear-view mirror, I thought I saw Alex quickly shake his head and mouth the word "Don't"—but I wasn't sure.

"Mom and Dad were fed up with L.A.," Rita went on after a few minutes. "They couldn't keep up with the high rents; said they wanted to move someplace simpler. I felt okay about coming here, but Alex—"

Alex reached forward and touched her shoulder. Rita clamped her mouth shut and smiled, turning around to look at him. "Sorry," she said. "I know, I know; I should shut up and let you speak for yourself, right?"

"Right." Alex sat back and huddled against the door. I kept my eyes fixed on the road; the curves were nasty on this part of the hill.

"Griswold must seem pretty small, after L.A.," I said, trying to make conversation.

"*Small*. That's putting it mildly," Alex muttered.

Rita laughed. "Come on, Alex, it's not so bad," she said. "We have a nice house. Even though the old lady next door's a little strange."

Alex winced. "I'd say more than a 'little' strange. Her house looks like it might fall down any second. She's got a Chevrolet that's about forty years old—and I don't think she has a regular bathroom—there's an outhouse in the back yard."

I laughed. "Lucky you. You're living next to Crazy Sadie."

"Crazy? What's wrong with her?" Rita asked.

"Nothing," I said. "That's just what some people call her, because of all the junk she has lying around, and the way she acts, I guess. Actually, she's my cousin. My sister says she's not so bad, once you get to know her."

Rita stared at me. "That woman's your *cousin*?"

"Supposedly. She's related to my grandmother."

"That's funny." Rita laughed.

I didn't think it was so funny. Why should they insult my relatives, *and* my town, when they'd just moved in? Of course, my best friend Sandy and I had pretty much decided we'd be out of Griswold right after graduation. Then Sandy beat me to it by going to Europe with his dad for three months. The creep.

As we rounded the last corner, Rita said, "There's our house. Better slow down, or my mom will have a fit."

Just as I thought: their place was the brown chalet. I wheeled into the driveway and left the engine running; I wasn't planning to stick around. "My dad built your house," I said.

Alex sat forward. "Is he a carpenter?"

"Uh-huh." I didn't tell him how much Dad hated this chalet; how he'd complained the design was hideous and that the architect, some guy from New Jersey, didn't know anything about roof pitches or Vermont winters. Right now the place was a mess; no one had cut the grass all summer. Boxes were stacked in the driveway and a couch sat outside the front door.

"Want to come in?" Rita asked. "You could meet my mom."

"Sorry," I said, "but I have to get home. Maybe another time."

"Sure," Rita said. "Thanks for the ride." She waved and went off toward the house. Alex got his stuff from the back and surprised me by coming to my window. His face was frozen like a statue in a wax museum, except for his lip, which quivered under his pale, fuzzy mustache.

"Who's this guy Randy?" Alex demanded.

I hesitated. "Tovitch?" I asked carefully. "He lives a few miles from here—he was our top scorer, as a junior. He can be funny, but he's also full of himself—"

"He doesn't like me," Alex said in a flat voice.

What could I say? The guy was right. "He's a little weird, that's all," I said. (As if I knew how to handle Tovitch. Who was I kidding?) "He's always been like that," I went on. "My dad said I should just ignore him— you know how parents talk." Alex winced, and I couldn't help laughing. "Sound familiar?"

He nodded. There didn't seem to be anything else to say, so I gave him a small wave and put the car in gear. "See you tomorrow."

Alex touched my arm, then quickly drew his hand away. "You play a good game of soccer," he said, and left before I could thank him.

I turned around slowly, in case their mother was watching, and took the first corner carefully, then I speeded up. I listened to music with one arm propped on the door, but I couldn't get the twins out of my mind. Rita was all right, I decided. But there was something different about Alex; I didn't know what it was. Suddenly, Randy's words weaseled their way into my brain: *Watch out for lover boy.* I rubbed my arm where Alex had touched it, and twisted the knob on the tape deck until "My Sweet One" was playing at top volume.

"Calm down," I said out loud. "Don't let Tovitch get to you. He's just jealous."

Jealous. That was it. I double-clutched into third, taking it easy on the corners. Tovitch was jealous of Alex, and I was too. Who wouldn't be, watching the way Beekman handled the ball, his moves on the field? He was a genius, I decided—maybe that's what made him seem strange.

I left it at that, and sang all the way home, my free foot thumping the floor, my open palm pounding the dash, until my voice was hoarse and my head was clear again.

# *Chapter Three*

I turned into our driveway and downshifted on the hill. I was tempted to rev the engine and spin out, but if Blair saw me, she'd take the keys in a flash. I parked under the maple tree and dropped my soccer gear near the pasture, spooking the sheep as usual. Crisco, our old collie, was sleeping under the porch; she thumped her tail as I climbed the steps. "Lazy bones," I said, and went into the kitchen, letting the screen door slam.

My sister Molly was sitting at the kitchen table, reading a letter. She slid it under a book, her face turning beet red the way mine did when I was in junior high and Blair discovered my *Playboy* magazines under the mattress.

"Another letter from Romeo?" I asked.

"None of your business," Molly said, sticking her nose in the air.

"Well, excuse *me*." I grabbed a peach from the fruit bowl. Obviously the letter was from Ramon. Who else would make her act that way? Ramon was the guy Molly met this summer when she decided, out of the blue, to go to California and solve the mystery of what Ashley, our mother, was doing out there when she died. Our mom's accident was so many years ago, I didn't understand why Molly got so obsessed with it. After she came back, with lots of mysteries solved (according to her, anyway), we had to live with Molly's puffed-up ego, *and* the fact that she'd found a boyfriend in some rinky-dink mining town.

It was hard to believe. My sister—who never had a date or even a phone call from a boy before, although she's not *that* bad looking—got letters from Ramon all the time. The whole thing was weird. Who'd go out with a guy who lived on the other side of the country? Oh, well, maybe it was smarter than what I was doing: dating my sister's oldest friend.

I was about to go upstairs when I noticed something else on the table—my math book from last year, and a sheet of paper beside it, covered with problems.

"What's this?" I asked, picking it up.

"Math," Molly said.

"Obviously." I let the paper drift down onto the table. "You're doing *math*, on summer vacation? Guess you like punishing yourself."

Molly tucked her hair behind her ears, and gave me that look that makes me feel she can see right into my brain. "If I'm going to be a scientist, I need to do better in math."

I shook my head. We'd been through this before. "Well, if you want to be a science nerd, I guess that's your choice." I went to the pantry for chips and popped open a bag, scanning the shelves for something more interesting to eat.

"If I'm a nerd, then Mom was too," Molly called from the table.

Our mom was a geologist, so Molly had me on that one. I wandered back into the room, munching chips. Molly scrambled to hide her letter again, but this time I was too fast for her. A picture fell on the floor, and before she could pick it up, I grabbed it and danced to the other side of the room.

"Give me that!" she yelped. I pushed her away from me while I studied the photo.

"Tsk, tsk," I said. "This is very cozy." There she was, my kid sister, sandy hair falling over one eye, bony knees showing, cuddled up against this guy with dark, olive-colored skin and spiked black hair—his arm draped around Molly's shoulder like he owned her.

"Whew!" I whistled. "Look at this. My sister, the future scientist, gone bananas over a guy!"

"Give it to me, you creep!" She dug her nails into my arm. I tossed the picture on the table.

"How old is this Ramon, anyway?" I asked.

"What do you care?" She held the picture to her chest. "All you do is make fun of him. Wait until he comes to visit—then you'll see."

"Comes to visit?" I choked. "Since when?"

She stuffed the picture and the letter into the envelope and picked up her book. "As soon as he has the money," she snapped, and went out on the porch, letting the door slam.

I shook my head. It was hard to figure what the guy

saw in her. Molly was flat chested, skinny, and so intense, it was exhausting. And now, with her fixation on
being a scientist . . . I crumpled the empty bag and
slam-dunked it into the trash. Who cared about Ramon,
anyway? It would be years before he showed up—and by
then I'd be long gone.

I took a quart of juice from the fridge and guzzled it
down, then looked out the window. Someone was biking
up the driveway; the minute I saw the short, blue-black
hair I knew it was Kai. She jumped off and walked up the
last, steep stretch, then dropped her bike under the
maple tree. Her dangling earrings flashed in the sun
when she waved to Molly.

I went outside with a goofy smile on my face, wishing
I could kiss her.

"Psst," I hissed at Molly. "Feel like going upstairs?"

"Why should I?" she answered in a perfectly loud
voice. "Kai's here to see me."

"Bull," I said, and went down the steps to meet Kai,
expecting her flashy grin. Instead I got a look so cool it
would make an engine seize up.

"I waved to you once already today, but I guess you
were going too fast to notice," Kai told me.

I froze on the bottom step, my neck prickling. "Oh?
Where were you?"

She held up her sleeves, streaked with orange and
yellow paint. "At work, painting scenery outside the
theater." Her black eyes got narrow and sharp, like ar-
rowheads. "You didn't even notice your own girlfriend.
Too busy looking at the stunning girl in the front seat,
right?"

*Stunning.* She'd picked a good word for Rita. I scooped up my soccer ball and kicked it over the railing. "You must have seen the Beekmans," I said, trying to sound casual. "Alex and his twin sister Rita are new in town; they both play soccer. They live just up the road, so I gave them a ride home. They're from L.A.—"

"You learned a lot in a short ride," Kai said.

"Give me a break. Can't I be friendly and help someone out? It was no big deal."

"Oh, really?" Kai tossed her head, then unwrapped a stick of gum and shoved it into her mouth, chewing hard.

Molly laughed from where she was sitting on the porch swing, and I glared up at her. "Back off, will you?" I said.

"Yeah," Kai said. "What's so funny?"

"*You* guys." Molly shoved her feet against the painted deck, rocking back and forth. She looked at Kai, then me. "What's the big deal about rides? Randy Tovitch brought me home last week, but that doesn't mean I'm going out with him."

I was so surprised, I didn't even notice that she'd bailed me out. "You rode with Tovitch? What are you, suicidal?" I asked.

Molly shook her head. "I was tired. It was a day when my ever-reliable brother was *supposed* to pick me up in town, but forgot." She hit me with her most accusing look. "Randy was perfectly polite. And he wasn't drunk, *or* stoned," she added quickly, as if she knew that would be my next question.

Kai laughed. "So I shouldn't worry about a gorgeous girl in Todd's car?"

"Right," I said, hoping my face wasn't too red.

"Just keep it that way," Kai warned, shoving my chest. She climbed up the steps and plopped down next to Molly. "Good; let's forget it. No big deal, like you said."

I grinned at her, then reached for my ball. One great thing about Kai: When she was done being mad, she was done, unlike my sister, who remembered every nasty crime I'd ever committed.

"Now, let's get to the important stuff," Kai said, as I sat down on the railing. "Who are these twins, anyway? Are they nice?"

"Sure," I said. "I guess so. I mean, I just met them."

"Why would they leave L.A. for Vermont?" Kai sounded like Alex, who obviously thought his parents had picked the weirdest place in the world to live.

"How should I know?" I asked. "Why do *you* leave Boston every summer to come here? Is there something wrong with this town?"

"Not really," Kai said, trying to calm me down. Molly told me once that Kai couldn't wait until she was old enough to spend her summers "someplace more interesting than Griswold."

"Don't get mad," Kai went on. "It just seems unusual to come here from Los Angeles. I mean, you know how it is; everyone always talks about L.A. like it's the ultimate place to go, the town where the surfers and movie stars live."

She had a point. "Rita said something about cheaper rents," I said. "If you need to know all the details about why the Beekmans are here, you'll have to ask them yourself."

"Maybe I will," Kai said, holding her knees. Her tight jeans showed every curve in her legs.

I stood up. "I doubt that Alex is a surfer or a movie star," I said, "but he sure plays a mean game of soccer. He was the lead scorer on his team out there—I even heard him say something to Craig about making a hat trick last season."

"A hat trick?" Kai cocked her head, puzzled. "What's that?"

"Three goals in one game," Molly said. I raised my eyebrows. *My* sister, keeping up with soccer? I thought she only knew about cross-country running, which was her thing—a good fit for her loner personality.

"So, that will be nice, having another good player," Kai said.

I frowned. "Maybe." I didn't feel like going into any more details right then. "Guess where they live?" I told Molly. "In that ugly chalet Dad built, next to Sadie's."

"Oh, good. It will be nice for Sadie to have neighbors," Molly said.

"I suppose. If they feel like talking to her."

Molly sat up straight and crossed her arms over her chest. "Why shouldn't they? Sadie's perfectly nice."

I sighed. "She's an ornery old bird, Mol. Admit it."

"Lighten up, you two." Kai skipped down the steps, kicked the soccer ball into the field, and linked her arm through mine. "Come on, Mr. Soccer Star. Molly and I are biking to the lake—want to come?"

"Maybe later," I said. "My legs are killing me—I'd never make it. I need a shower and lunch. Why don't you stay and keep me company?"

"Sorry," Kai said, "but Mol and I have made plans. If I run into any good-looking guys, I'll let you know." She cocked her head and smiled.

"Give me a break," I said. "You know I'm the best in town."

Molly snorted and went for the door. "I'll get my suit," she said.

I had Kai behind the maple tree in a second. I leaned back against the rough bark and pulled her close, kissing her until I was out of breath. And I have to hand it to my sister; she was upstairs long enough so I even had time to slip my hand under Kai's shirt. When Molly came back out, she let the door slam, and Kai jerked away. She looked pretty calm, but my face was burning up.

"See you," Kai said, tossing me a little wave. I watched her pedal down the hill, with Molly right behind, then went inside. Too late, I remembered that Randy and his friends were hanging out at the lake. He'd better not come on to Kai. She looked great in a bikini.

"Cool it," I told myself, heading upstairs. "Tovitch isn't a problem. It's just those new kids in town. They've fried your brains."

I stripped down, turned on the shower, and stood there for a long time, letting the cool water soothe me all the way down.

# Chapter Four

"Pass, O'Connor, out to the side—I'm open!" Tovitch shouted from the wing.

"Man on, Todd, man on!" Someone was breathing hard behind me. I scrambled, dodged right, then dribbled a few more steps down the center of the field, glancing to the left and forward. Tovitch called to me again, but a J.V. fullback was rushing to mark him. I kept going. Alex came out of nowhere and raised his hand to show me he was clear. I kicked the pass with my right foot. Alex trapped it and ran down the field, dodging two more defensive players.

"Alex, over to me!" Tovitch surged toward the middle as they neared the goal, and Alex shot the ball across to him. But Tovitch was guarded on all sides; he almost tripped over a J.V. sweeper. In the confusion of feet and bodies, the goalie ran out, grabbed the ball, and booted it back down the field before Tovitch could get his foot on it.

"Come on, Alex, try aiming it," Tovitch snarled, as we wheeled to follow the play behind us.

"He *did* aim it. That kid on defense was just too fast for you," I grumbled. Tovitch glared at me, spit angrily, and jogged ahead, but slowly. He was off today, sluggish. He gasped for breath as we crossed the center line. Of course, I wasn't exactly sailing. Playing midfield, I'd been running nonstop since the first whistle blew, and the sweat was pouring off me. It was Friday, the fifth day of practice, our last scrimmage with both teams together. Starting Monday, the J.V. would be practicing on their own—and so would we.

The ball went out for a corner kick. Crawford blew the whistle for subs and sent Drew in for Dexter on right wing. The coach tapped a few more sophomores, who trotted in looking pretty nervous—their last chance to make varsity.

"Todd, Alex, Randy—any of you guys want a rest?" Crawford called.

I shook my head, even though my lungs felt as if someone had filled them with old socks. "I'm fine, coach," Tovitch yelled, jogging up beside me. He jabbed me in the ribs. "What's the deal anyway, always passing it to Beekman?"

I scrubbed my hair with both hands. "Hey, he was in the open. You had a man on."

"I don't play *wing*," Tovitch muttered. "At least, I didn't until today. Stupid Beekman. He's got Crawford in his back pocket. First Alex takes your position, then mine—it sucks."

I jogged slowly in place, waiting for a throw-in. "Half-back's not so bad," I said, even though I'd rather be on the front line. "Besides, Crawford said no one's position is definite until we get to the first game. I'm sure he'll put you back at striker."

"He'd better." Tovitch sounded as if he'd paste some-one if it turned out different.

"Hey, with Alex on the team, we might make the play-offs for once," I reminded him.

"Maybe." Tovitch lowered his voice. "But I'm not giv-ing my spot to a guy who's not even a *guy*—if you know what I mean. Look at him run—see? Like a girl, with his hands up—oooh!"

Tovitch minced down the field with his hands turned up at his waist.

I couldn't help laughing, even though Alex didn't really run like that. In fact, I was jealous of the way Beekman moved—his limbs seemed fluid and oiled; I felt stiff and awkward beside him.

"Todd, yours!" Craig booted the ball from the back-field. I should have headed it, but I wasn't paying atten-tion. A J.V. player beat me to it, took it on the chest, and kicked it back down toward our goal.

"Wake up!" Crawford shouted. "This is a scrimmage, not a jam session!"

Damn Tovitch. His obsession with Alex was spoiling my game. When Crawford pulled us both off the field a few seconds later, I felt as if we'd been punished. I drank about six cups of water, tossed my cup on the grass, and sank onto the bench, rubbing my thighs to ease the stiff-ness that was setting in already. But I didn't have a second's peace. Someone tapped my shoulder and said, "Well, well, if it isn't the King of Sweat himself."

I wheeled around. Kai was standing behind me, her face made up as if she were about to go onstage: blue eye shadow, mascara, rosy cheeks, long dangling earrings—the works. She was sloppy from the neck down, though; her tie-dyed shirt and cutoffs were splattered with paint. "Hey, Kai, what's up?" I asked as I swiveled back to watch the field. If Crawford saw her, I was screwed.

"Nothing much. Still painting scenery. I've been here for a while, but you didn't notice."

"How could I? I was playing the game." Kai should know better than to hang around our practice. I jumped up and edged away from the bench so the other guys wouldn't listen; a few were snickering already. "I can't talk now—Crawford gives us a hard time if we don't pay attention, even when we're off the field."

"I get the picture." Kai blew a bubble, almost in my face.

"Come on, Kai," I whispered. "Crawford makes the final cuts this weekend. I don't want to blow my chances."

"*So* sorry to bother you," she said, crossing her arms tight over her chest.

"What are you doing later?" I asked. "I'll be done soon—"

"I might go to the lake," she said. "Dad's coming from Boston tonight, so I have to be home."

"Can we get together?"

She cocked her head to the side. "I'll see what's up, okay?" Her eyes were as cool as her voice. I tried to watch the guys on the field, but she was sure distracting. "Anyway," she went on, "it sounds as though you're always busy after practice, giving *certain* people rides."

"Come on, Kai; we went through this the other day. Besides, I've only taken them twice—"

But Kai was on her way, her bum switching a little as she waved to some guys on the football squad. I dug the heel of my cleat in the grass, tearing up the sod. Why'd I have to pick the prickliest girl in town to be my girlfriend?

Tovitch chuckled behind me. "Problems?"

I whirled around. "Yeah. Girls." I managed a laugh. "Kai's uptight because I've given Rita two rides home. Big deal."

Randy's bushy eyebrows drew into a straight line. "Rita's nice to look at," he said. "Trouble is, if you hang out with one, you get the other one too."

I bounced in place to keep warm, watching the play. "Beekman's all right—hey, look at that." The ball was high in the air; Alex came out of nowhere and ran to meet it, setting his neck and then snapping his forehead straight into the ball for a header that shot right over to Drew. The sophomore stopped it with his chest and spurted up the field. "Nice move, huh?" I said.

Tovitch nodded. "He's got amazing ball control. But—"

"But what?" I glanced at Tovitch. His face twisted into an ugly grin.

"He's missing plenty somewhere else." Tovitch pointed at his crotch, then laughed.

"You're gross," I told him.

"Sure," he said. "But so are fags."

I froze. "Who says Alex is a fag?"

Tovitch snickered. "Wake up, O'Connor. Just watch him move. He's wimpy."

As if he'd heard us, Crawford shouted from the sidelines, "Beekman, challenge him! Get aggressive!"

"See?" Tovitch demanded.

I shrugged. "Come on, Crawford says that to everyone."

Tovitch shook his head. "Not me."

I laughed. "Right. Just what we need is you being *more* aggressive, picking up yellow cards and fouls."

Tovitch grinned, showing that jagged tooth. Obviously I'd said the right thing, playing to his macho image. The whistle blew at last, and he kept his trap shut until the coach waved a few players off the field. "Drew, Alex, Craig, take a rest," Crawford said, and beckoned to us. "Todd, Randy, play front line; Todd, left wing; Randy, striker."

Tovitch hooted and punched my arm as we trotted onto the field. "That's more like it. We'll show Crawford this time."

We didn't do so well at first, playing boom ball with the J.V., each side smashing it up and down the field without much direct passing. Crawford got agitated. His thin blond hair was plastered to his forehead and his face was red, as if he were running the field himself. "Don't just kick it!" he yelled. "Trap the ball! Pass it to a player, not the sky. Control! Control!"

Finally Craig booted it up to the right, and Drew was on it, his body so low to the ground, I couldn't believe he could run that fast. He took the pass and sent it across to Tovitch. A defensive man stopped the ball and passed to the left, but I was there. I chipped it back to the center and Tovitch kicked it straight at the goal. The J.V. keeper lunged sideways but missed, and the ball bounced from the post right into the net.

"All *right!*" I yelled. Tovitch raised his hand to slap me five, then hit Drew.

"Nice one!" Drew said.

I beamed. My first assist. "See what we can do together if we keep that *girl* on the bench?" Tovitch laughed softly.

"Girl?" Drew's innocent face was puzzled. "What are you talking about?"

"Don't tell me you haven't noticed?" Tovitch asked. "Sorry—I forgot you're too young to know about this stuff."

"Lay off, Tovitch," I said. Drew shook his head, confused, and trotted out to the right.

That was our only goal; the J.V. held us for the last few minutes of the game. I glanced at Crawford when the game was over, hoping for a compliment, but the coach was busy with Drew. When Crawford clapped his shoulder, Drew's grin spread over his face like spilled paint. He's made the team, I thought, and smiled with him, knowing how good that must feel inside.

The coach pulled us together for a few minutes. "Good workout," he told us. "Freshmen and sophomores, don't be disappointed if you stay on junior varsity. You'll be stronger players next year."

The younger guys looked at the ground; a few shot jealous glances at Drew, who couldn't keep the grin off his face. "I'll call everyone on the weekend," Crawford said. "Go home and get some rest, and be here early Monday morning. J.V. practices on the lower field."

I smiled at Craig. "Nice to be on the big field for once."

He frowned. "Assuming we're on the team."

"What do you mean?" I whispered. "You're on. Who else can play sweeper?"

He gave me a quick smile. "Thanks. Hope you're right." He slapped my shoulder as he turned to go. "Have a good weekend."

"Yeah, you too."

I watched him leave, then pulled off my shin guards and unlaced my cleats, standing up slowly. Everything hurt.

"Nice assist." Alex came up beside me, speaking so softly I barely heard him.

I gave him a quick smile, my eyes roving around to see if Tovitch was still in sight. Luckily he was on the way to his truck on the far side of the lot. "Thanks," I said. "We should have had another one, too, when you passed it off to Randy."

Alex raised his hands. "Next time."

"Sure." I grabbed my stuff and hustled to my car, praying Alex wouldn't beg a ride. But the girls weren't done yet; he walked over to their field, waiting for Rita, I assumed.

"Hey, O'Connor!" I glanced around. Tovitch waved

from his truck, revving his engine as Dexter climbed in. "It's Friday. Time to party," he called. "Come to the lake."

"Maybe later," I said, waving back, but he couldn't have heard. He squealed out of the lot and took the corner on two wheels, barely missing some little kid on a bike. "Idiot," I thought, glad I wasn't relying on *him* for rides.

When I got home, I stripped off my shirt, tossed it on the grass, and doused myself with the hose, aiming the nozzle right at my head. The water was icy cold; I did a little dance under the blast and didn't even notice that Blair had come outside until I saw her bare feet through the stream of water.

"Rough practice?" she called.

I hosed my legs, then closed the nozzle. "Hi, Blair." My stepmother had that fuzzy look that meant she'd been in the darkroom too long.

"How's it going?" she asked.

"Fine." I wiped my eyes with the back of my arm and glanced at her, checking her mood. "Mind if I take the car to the lake?"

"Not at all. As long as Molly goes along, too—and make sure she's got a ride to her practice from there."

"No problem."

I made myself a sandwich, changed into my bathing suit, and finished the juice in the plastic pitcher, ignoring the drips down the front of my chest. When I came outside, the Subaru was at the bottom of the driveway, lurching across the bridge. It nosed onto the road, then turned around in slow motion. Blair was sitting in the porch swing, watching. "Good thing no one's coming," she said, chuckling.

I perched on the railing, flicking my towel at the geraniums. "Don't," Blair said automatically.

I quit, and stared at the Subaru, shaking my head. "Molly's blocking the whole road. Aren't you afraid she'll have an accident?"

"She's doing all right. Remember how many times you drove up and down the driveway before you got your license?"

"Yeah." In fact, it had seemed like an eternity until the day I finally turned sixteen. But my kid sister Molly at the wheel? Forget it.

"So how's practice going?" Blair asked again. "You haven't said much about it."

"Pretty good." I took a swig of water from the bottle I was carrying. "I think I'll be starting. Crawford's calling us tomorrow."

"Great!" Blair's green eyes danced as if *she* were the one making the team. "I'm not surprised, of course; you played so well last year. What position?"

I frowned. "I'm not sure yet. There's this new guy, Alex Beekman. He's really good—better than I could ever be. He'll be on the front line for sure, so I may end up in the midfield."

Blair was quiet for a minute. "Did you say his name was Beekman? I think I met his mother in town yesterday. Are they in the chalet, next to Sadie's?"

"Yeah. They're from L.A."

Blair nodded. "No wonder she seemed so lonesome—

that's a long way from home. I don't think she's ever lived in the country before. Is there a Mr. Beekman?"

"He's coming in a few weeks."

"I should ask them over," Blair said, pushing at the floor until the swing started moving.

My chest tightened. "Do you have to?"

Blair looked puzzled. "Of course I don't *have* to, but it's a neighborly thing to do. Is her son so bad?"

*Just a fag,* I almost said. I bit my lip and took a slow breath, stalling. "Maybe you could invite Mrs. Beekman for lunch, when we're not here. I don't want to have to entertain her kids."

"Kids?" she asked. "How many Beekmans are there?"

"Two. Alex has a twin sister, Rita."

"Is *she* the problem?"

"No!" I said. "It's just something—I can't explain."

"Sounds mysterious." Blair let her hair down, twisted it into a coil, and clipped it again, but she kept her eyes on my face, waiting for more information. Luckily Molly saved me by roaring up the driveway and stalling right in front of the house. The car coughed and lurched forward. I laughed.

"Don't say anything!" Molly ordered, leaning out the window.

I hopped over the railing and leaned against the driver's door. "Playing my Tull tape, huh?" I asked, hearing flute music fluttering from the speakers.

"It was sitting in the car," Molly said.

I tossed my towel in the back, opened the door, and jostled her shoulder. "Move over."

She gave me a cool, steady look. "Why? Where are we going?"

"To the lake. Go on, get your suit."

"I'm wearing it." Molly didn't budge. Her hands gripped the steering wheel as if they were covered with glue. "Can't I drive to the road?"

"No." I poked her, harder this time. "Let go."

"Todd—" Blair warned, but Molly was scooting over.

"Yes, *sir*," Molly said, saluting as she lifted her knees over the gearshift. Okay legs, I thought, but not as nice as Rita's. I waved to Blair, jammed the car into first, and headed down the hill. The old planking rumbled as we crossed the bridge.

"In exactly one year I'll be driving on my own," Molly announced.

"In one year I'll have my own wheels—if I'm lucky."

"Wow. Aren't you cool." She glanced at my feet. "Don't you wear shoes when you drive?"

"When I feel like it." Molly would never understand what a charge I got, feeling that smooth rubber ribbing under my soles, connecting me to the engine. Anyway, cars were just convenient machines, to Molly. To me, they had personalities. I even played a game, matching people and animals to vehicles.

Take Dad's truck, for instance. It was slow and old; you could say it was like Crisco, our stiff old dog. The Subaru was more like me—scruffy and noisy. And then there was my favorite car in the world—the sweet, speedy BMW. Sleek—like Rita Beekman, I thought. I grinned, wondering if Rita would like being compared to a Beemer. Probably not. And if Rita was a Beemer, what was Kai? I was searching my brain for a fast, glittering sports car when Molly asked, "What's so funny?"

"Nothing," I said, secretly continuing my game. I glanced at my sister. If Molly were a car, what would she be? A Volvo, I decided. Boring, but dependable. I laughed to myself.

"Come on, tell me the joke," Molly insisted.

But I just shook my head. There were some things girls would never understand.

# Chapter Five

The lake was crowded, but I spotted Kai right away, lounging at the end of the dock in her bright purple bikini. When Molly waved to her, Kai wiggled one foot in our direction. I stopped and stared. Was she talking to Tovitch? I bristled, snapping my towel.

When I got closer, I realized for the first time that Kai and Randy looked alike, with their dark, thick hair cut short; their olive skin and black eyes. But their personalities were totally different. "Hey, Kai," I said, ignoring Tovitch.

She flashed me a quick smile. Apparently she'd quit being mad.

"Hi, Todd." Randy's eyes were glued to Kai's chest. I followed his leer and realized he could see right down the top of Kai's suit—just where I'd put my hand the other day.

I felt a sudden bulge in my trunks and turned away. "Time for a swim." I ran to the end of the dock, dove into the lake, and stroked as fast as I could out beyond the roped-in swimming area. The cold water calmed me down. I swam a long way, then drifted back and hoisted myself up onto the raft, waiting for a bunch of little kids to jump off. When they were gone, I climbed the rickety ladder to the tower and glanced toward the shore. The raft rocked; it was a long way down. Should I jump, or dive? I decided on a jackknife, and hoped Kai was watching, because my dive felt clean and crisp. I went deep, arched my back just before I hit the murky bottom, and shot to the surface.

When I popped out of the water, shaking my head and gasping for breath, someone called, "Hi, Todd!"

I looked up. Rita Beekman was standing on the tower, gripping the railing. From below, she looked like one smooth, long leg. Her hair was in a tight braid dangling over one shoulder, and the sun glinted off her wet arms. I stayed put, treading water. "Come on, jump," I said. "It's not too far."

She raised her arms a couple of times, trying it out, then turned, balanced her toes on the lip, and did a perfect back dive from the edge, slicing into the water right beside me. "Hey," I complained, paddling backward quickly and sputtering. "Trying to kill me?"

"Sorry," she said. "It's cold compared to the pool where we used to swim."

"You had a pool in L.A.?" I asked.

Rita shook her head. "No, but our neighbors did, with a hot tub at one end."

"Sounds like the movies," I said.

"Not really." We were swimming toward shore now, doing the breaststroke. "Most of L.A.'s not like the movies. It's just big and regular. Except it has the ocean."

I laughed. "Regular, but not like Griswold."

Rita didn't answer. She took a few more strokes and said, "I met your friend Kai."

"Yeah?" We could touch bottom, now. I stood up and slicked my hair back.

"She's nice," Rita said, ringing out her braid. "How long have you two been going out?"

"Not that long," I hedged. "We've known each other since we were little—she's my sister's best friend."

Rita glanced at me, her blue eyes curious. "She made it sound like more than that."

Good grief. Had she and Kai been having a heart-to-heart already?

"Sorry," Rita said quickly. "Alex hates it when I get so nosy. I'd love to meet your sister. Is she here?"

"On the dock." We waded to shore and rubbed ourselves dry. Rita followed me to the dock. Molly was perched beside Kai, wearing her ratty bathing suit with a T-shirt over it. They were both giggling at something Tovitch had said; he was on the beach below them, untying a rowboat. I draped my towel over my shoulders and walked along the smooth planking, wishing Rita weren't tagging along, but what could I do? After all, I hadn't asked Rita to swim with me.

"Aren't you going to introduce us?" Rita asked, catching me off guard.

I blushed and made it quick. "Molly, this is Rita Beekman. Rita, my sister."

"Nice to meet you." Rita gave Molly one of her open

smiles and spread her towel beside my sister. Of course, she didn't know that Kai was watching her with that steady squint, which meant she was memorizing her every move and gesture. Kai didn't work at the theater for nothing; she was determined to end up onstage—where she'd probably do perfect imitations of us all. My sister was quiet, but I knew she wasn't missing a trick either. Meanwhile, Rita just talked and asked questions as if she'd been swimming at Griswold Lake since she was little.

"Hey, O'Connor." Tovitch swatted my ankle; his legs were braced while he bailed out the boat. "Dex and I are rowing to the big rock. Want to come?" Tovitch hoisted his backpack into the boat and stowed the oars in the oarlocks.

I hesitated. Was it better to stay on the dock with three girls who were driving me crazy, or hang out with a guy who made me nervous?

"Nice dive," said Kai suddenly.

"Thanks," I said, but she was complimenting Rita, not me. That settled it. "Sure, I'll come with you," I told Randy, and stepped into the bow seat just as they pushed off.

No one said much while Tovitch rowed down the lake, hugging the shore. Just past the tall pines we rounded the point and came to the long, sloping rock that pitched into deep water; a perfect place for diving. It was tricky, landing a boat there. Tovitch maneuvered as close as he could while I leaned forward, grabbed hold of the ledge, and scrambled out, holding the bow line. I sat with my legs dangling, steadying the boat while Dex and Tovitch climbed up, looping the rope around the trunk of a spindly tree.

"Going in?" I asked. The water was a dark slate-green, usually cold; the sun hit here only in the afternoons.

"No thanks," Tovitch said, rummaging in his pack. I took a long breath and dove deep, swimming through the shafts of sunlight until my lungs were bursting.

When I got out, shivering, Randy and Dex were sitting at the top of the ledge, rolling a joint. A plastic bag of marijuana lay open at their feet. I edged away, stretching out on the warm stone. Maybe if I pretended to be asleep, I could stay clear of them. I heard the flick of a match; smelled the sulphur and then the sweet marijuana fumes.

Tovitch nudged my leg. I opened my eyes. His lips were sealed tight as he held in the smoke. He waved the joint in my direction. "No thanks," I said.

Tovitch leaned over and exhaled in my face. "Okay, Mr. Clean Jeans. Whatever you say." He passed the joint to Dex, who took a deep toke, smiling and rolling his eyes.

"Now," Tovitch said when they'd passed it back and forth a few times, "Dex and I have something to tell you. We've decided it's time to do something about Beekman. Right, Dex?"

"Right." Dex gave him a bleary nod. He looked stoned already.

"Like what?" I asked, closing my eyes and trying to sound casual, as if it was no big deal.

Tovitch sucked in the smoke and said, between his

teeth, "You're a weird one, O'Connor. Don't you see what's happening?"

I sat up. "Sure. I see Alex taking the position I hoped to play. It's a drag—but I don't know why it should affect *you* so much. I'm the one that should be pissed."

"Yeah," Tovitch said. "You should be. So why aren't you? Or can I guess?"

He nudged Dex, who gave me an ugly sneer. I didn't like the way this conversation was going. I picked up a flat stone and sidearmed it across the water, counting the skips and keeping my face turned away. "Why's it such a big deal? There's room for eleven on the field—we can all play."

Tovitch snorted. "You sound like Miss Foster, back in kindergarten."

"Why are you so worked up about this?" I asked carefully. "Beekman's a great player. Just because Crawford put Alex in your position once—"

"Twice. Beekman played striker on Tuesday."

"And I played it on Wednesday. Big deal. So did Drew. Crawford's still moving everyone around, seeing where we fit."

"And what if he decides I don't fit at striker?" Tovitch said.

"Then you play wing. Or maybe he'll have four guys on the forward line."

"Maybe." Tovitch rubbed the joint out on the rock and tossed it into the water. "My idea is this," he said. "We do whatever it takes to get our positions back—"

"Hold on," I said. "We've only had a week of practice.

We don't even *have* positions yet. You've been a striker most of the time. I don't know if I'm starting—"

"You are," Tovitch said. "Right, Dex? Tell him what you saw."

Dexter shot me a sleepy look. His eyes were blood-shot now. "Crawford's list," he said. "He left his clip-board lying around."

"And?" I asked. Dex talked so slowly, he was annoying at the best of times. Now the dope made his voice sound like a tape playing at a slow speed.

"So, your name was on the starting list." Dex paused. "You . . . Craig . . . Drew . . . Randy . . . Alex—"

I grinned. I was psyched, of course. This was what I'd waited for all these years—not just to *make* varsity, but to start. "What about you?" I asked.

Dex wiped his nose with the side of his hand. "Question mark," he said.

"You'll make it," I told him, although I wondered. Dex tried hard, but sometimes he was clumsy, and the type who waited for someone—the coach, Tovitch, any-one else—to tell him what to do.

"Think about today," Randy said, sliding down the ledge until he was close to the lip. The bag of weed fluttered in the wind; Tovitch scooped it up and held it tight. "You know that goal we made together? That's the way it's meant to be—you and me on the front line, and Alex behind us."

"Where he doesn't play as well," I said. "Geez, To-vitch, you're as transparent as that Zip-loc bag. Sounds like you'd rather lose than see Alex score."

Tovitch gave me a long, dark stare. "Maybe you're tighter with Beekman than I thought," he said.

"Listen, Tovitch, I hardly know the guy. He's only been in town a few days!" My voice sounded shrill; I took a deep breath to steady it. Dex laughed, tossing a rock into the lake, and Tovitch leered at me, his black eyebrows wiggling.

"Sure, sure. But we could make it sound like something's happening. We might mention it to Kai—"

"What," I demanded. "What would you mention?"

"We might ask her why she hangs out with someone who likes *guys* instead of girls—"

"Jesus!" I exploded. "First you decide Alex is gay—for who knows what reason. Now *I'm* gay too? Is that it?"

Randy tossed me his nastiest smile. "Just something I might mention to the other guys on the team. Unless—"

"Unless what?" I clenched my fists and stepped closer. Randy stepped back, his heels near the edge of the rock, watching me carefully. "Unless you keep quiet about our getting stoned . . ." He shook the bag near my face. "And quit passing to Alex."

"You're nuts. That's suicide, for the team."

Randy whistled. "Listen to him, Dex. Can you believe the morality of this man?"

"Really." Dexter's face got twisted. "I've been wondering what goes on in O'Connor's car, haven't you, Tovitch?"

"Sure," Randy said. "The question is, does he come on to the sister or the brother?"

"Asshole." I lifted my fist. Tovitch took another step backward and slipped on the smooth stone. As he lost his balance, I gave him a shove and he went flying into the water, howling. He landed with a smack and the bag flew from his hand. Bright green shreds of marijuana fluttered in the breeze. The bag floated on the surface for a second, then slowly filled with water.

Dexter's mouth dropped open; he stumbled to his feet. "Hey!" he yelled. It was such a delayed reaction I had to laugh. Tovitch came up spluttering, treaded water for a second, then splashed awkwardly toward the rock.

"For such a fine athlete, you're a lousy swimmer," I called. I pointed at the bag, just going under. "Lost something?"

"We'll kill you for this," Randy cried. "Dexter, get him."

Dex lunged. I dodged and danced close to the edge of the diving rock. "Come on," I taunted and turned toward the water. A bright flash of sun glinted off metal, and I grinned. Kai, Molly, and Rita sat high in a big Grumman canoe, paddling straight down the lake before the wind.

"So long, guys," I said, and dove out over Randy's head, hitting the water hard with my chest and stroking away as fast as I could.

I swam without stopping; when I lifted my head to catch a breath, the canoe was waiting for me. Molly back-paddled in the stern, holding the boat steady while I swam close. Kai stretched out her paddle from the middle thwart but I ignored it, grabbing the gunwale. The canoe rocked and Rita squealed from her bow perch.

"Todd!" Molly yelled. "Cut it out! We'll capsize."

I steadied them, shaking my head to clear the water from my eyes. "Can I hitch a ride?" I asked Kai.

"What do you think?" Kai asked the others. "Shall we let him in?"

"No way," Molly said. "He'll overload the boat."

"We'll have to think about it," Rita said, laughing.

"Your choice," I said, yanking on the gunwale. "Let me in or I'll turn you over." The canoe tipped and bobbed.

"Todd!" they screamed.

I let go. "Kai, scoot back. Keep your paddles in the water," I told them. "I'm coming aboard."

I reached across, grabbed the far gunwale, and kicked hard. My belly scraped against the side as I flopped into the bottom like a hooked fish. The canoe rocked wildly, taking in water, then settled down.

"Show-off," Molly said.

I sat up, leaning against the metal thwart. "Home, James."

"Watch it," Rita said, twisting around on the seat to look down at me. "These girls don't take orders."

I rolled my eyes. "All right, all right. But let's go somewhere fast, or I'm finished."

Rita's blue eyes darkened to the color of the lake. "Why?" she asked.

"Just move it, okay? Actually, give me a paddle. Here, Kai, I'll take yours."

She handed it over. Molly turned the canoe and pointed us back down the lake. We dug in hard and the boat shuddered, bucking the wind. Tovitch scrambled onto the rock, stood up, and raised his fist, shouting. The waves slapping the bow drowned his words. Dex did a sloppy surface dive and came up empty-handed. I laughed and took another stroke.

"Did you push Randy in?" Kai asked.

"We were just fooling around," I said.

"It looked like you were fighting," Molly said.

"Maybe."

Kai ran her finger down my neck and leaned close to my ear. "What were you fighting about?" she asked in a soft voice.

I turned my head to the side so my mouth almost touched hers. "You," I whispered, and dug the paddle into the water.

Kai sat back, laughing. "Liar," she said.

I shrugged and left it at that.

# Chapter Six

I managed to get back to the boat house and into the Subaru before Tovitch showed up at the dock. By the time I dropped Molly at her practice and headed home, it was late afternoon. I took our hill too fast, and was so amazed by what I saw in the yard that I slammed on the brakes, nearly knocking my forehead against the windshield.

Right in front of the barn, parked near the open doors as if it belonged to us, was a sea-green BMW, clean and shiny in spite of being a few years old. I jumped out, not even bothering to shut the door, and headed straight for the Beemer. "Sweet," I said, running my hands along her sleek side.

The door was locked. I peered through the windows. Black leather seats, a little worn in places; tape deck with a cassette sticking out; sunglasses dangling from the rearview mirror—whose car? Not Dad's, with Massachusetts plates—unless he'd won the lottery or something. Besides, he was working on a job in New Hampshire. He'd been away all week and probably wasn't home yet. Must be someone visiting Blair.

"Swee-eet," I said again, whistling. So easy to imagine myself behind the wheel. I'd rev the engine, coax it down the driveway, and then take the corners at full speed—with the windows open and the radio blasting.

"Control yourself, will you?" I said out loud. "You don't even know who owns the thing." I whistled as I climbed the porch steps. This day might turn out all right after all.

A strange pair of sandals sat beside the door, but the kitchen was empty. I grabbed a can of soda, popped it open, and went into the family room. I blinked, adjusting to the dim light, and that's when I noticed the man stretched out on the couch. For a split second I thought it was Dad, but then I realized it was his younger brother, Gordo, a bigger version of my father. I stood there quietly, grinning. Life always got more interesting when Uncle Gordo was around—which didn't happen too often. And right now, Uncle Gordo on the couch and a BMW in the driveway could mean only one thing: It was his car. Unbelievable.

Uncle Gordo snored with his mouth open, his glasses propped on his forehead and his hands folded over his stomach. I was about to go back into the kitchen when he twitched, opened his eyes, and blinked at me.

"Todd!" He struggled to his feet, yawning, then pulled me into a bear hug before holding me at arm's length. "What did they do, attach you to a stretching machine? You're huge!"

Of course, no one's huge compared to my uncle, but I

didn't say that. "Hey, Uncle Gordo, when did you get here? I didn't know you were coming."

"Neither did anyone else," he said. "I decided to surprise you. The house was as silent as a tomb when I arrived, so I fell asleep." He ran his hands through his long hair, untucking the tangles from his collar.

"Nice car," I said, grinning.

He shrugged. "Hey, what can I say? My neighbor was desperate to sell. It's in great shape, even though it's six years old, and it's got low mileage."

"Looks excellent."

"Of course. You've got cars on your mind all the time, right?"

I nodded, and Uncle Gordo grinned. "I was impossible at your age. Actually, I'm not sure I ever quit." He shoved his glasses up onto his nose and slumped back down on the couch, patting the cushions; I sat beside him.

"Is Gary here?" I asked. Gary is Uncle Gordo's partner in a fish restaurant they run on the Cape.

He shook his head. "Things were too busy for both of us to leave. I had no business running off, but Gary realized I had to give the new car a trial run, so he told me to beat it for a few days. I thought I'd better visit my favorite niece and nephew."

Uncle Gordo always calls us that: his favorite niece and nephew. Of course, he doesn't have any others, but so what? I took a drink of soda and offered him the can. He sipped and passed it back.

"So what are you up to?" he asked. "Still kicking that ball around the field?"

"Yeah—I'm trying out for varsity this year."

He laughed. "What do you mean, 'trying out'? You'll make the team, won't you?"

"Probably. But I want to be first-string."

"Of course," he said, "who wouldn't? I'd love to come to a game—if you could stand to hear your loudmouth uncle roaring from the sidelines."

"No problem," I said. "We can always use the support."

I settled against the arm of the couch, studying him. Uncle Gordo was wearing a black T-shirt with Rock Ovens—the name of his restaurant—stenciled on the front. Except for his hair, speckled with gray, he looked like a kid, with his bare feet, worn-out jeans, and one gold earring. "So the restaurant's busy?" I asked.

Uncle Gordo leaned back and patted his stomach. "Very. As you can see, Gary's food is still superb. But the Cape is crazy. Someday one car too many will drive over the Sagamore Bridge. Cape Cod will shear away from the mainland and go groaning out to sea. Gary and I will keep serving people until the food's gone, and then abandon ship."

I smiled at the thought of Provincetown, and Uncle Gordo's restaurant, floating across the Atlantic while Gary cooked lobsters and Uncle Gordo cruised the dining room, talking to the customers as if they were all his best friends.

Uncle Gordo stood up, stretched, and pulled his T-shirt down over his belly. "No one's home?"

"I'm not sure—Blair's probably in the darkroom. She's working on a big project."

He nodded. "Her pictures get better all the time. I couldn't believe it when her photo made the cover of *Cape Cod* magazine." He tugged his hair and grinned at me. "Want to check out the car?"

I'm sure my smile must have spread from one ear to the other. "Great."

We went outside. "You got your license, right?" Uncle Gordo asked.

I nodded. "Last winter."

He poked me in the ribs. "It's fabulous, isn't it?" He glanced around the yard, lowering his voice as if we were plotting something illegal. "How about a trial run before your dad gets home?"

I opened my mouth, then shut it. "That would be amazing. You don't mind?"

He shook his head. "Long as you stick to the speed limit, and let *me* choose the music."

"Deal." I wiped my hands on the seat of my pants; they were sweaty from excitement.

Uncle Gordo unlocked the driver's door, reached over to the other side, and motioned me in. "I'll drive the first few minutes, show you the ropes. Then we'll trade."

The car smelled clean, even though it wasn't new. The seats were low and comfortable. The dashboard gleamed; someone, probably Uncle Gordo, had polished all the dials and knobs. We put on our belts, and Uncle Gordo drove slowly down the driveway, showing me the gears, pointing out the tachometer, the hand brake, and a whole lot of other stuff that I already knew about, but I still listened carefully.

Uncle Gordo stayed on the back roads, heading uphill

toward the Beekmans. We took a sharp corner pretty fast, but the wheels gripped the gravel—not like the Subaru, which always fishtailed in that spot. Uncle Gordo grinned. "Handles like a dream, doesn't it?" He pulled over, shut the engine off, and climbed out. "Your turn."

We traded places. For a second I was almost too nervous to drive. What if I screwed up? But Uncle Gordo just waited quietly; he wasn't tense the way Dad would have been. The car was jerky at first; it took me a while to get the feel of the gears.

"It's so much smoother than the Subaru," I said, finding my way from second to third. We passed the Beekmans' and I slowed down, hoping Rita might be outside, but the yard was empty. Damn; missed my chance. We kept climbing to the top of the hill, past Sadie's and onto the straightaway. I eased the Beemer into fourth; the engine hummed steadily, and I gripped the wheel, feeling its power under my hands and feet, just waiting to be set loose. "This is unbelievable," I said softly. "It's amazing you let me do this."

Uncle Gordo clapped my shoulder and laughed. "My pleasure. Besides, you're a good driver."

A few miles on, the road narrowed to a single track, and we turned around. It would have been so easy to speed down the hill, but I stayed in control. Uncle Gordo hummed under his breath, then shoved a tape into the deck. I smiled; it was Bob Marley singing "Talking Blues." "I love that album," I said.

Uncle Gordo crossed his arms and settled back in his seat. "Great minds think alike." He sang along, but I was too busy concentrating on the curves to join in.

I could have driven all night, but of course we reached our driveway much too soon and Uncle Gordo motioned for me to go across the bridge. I turned in, then slowed down, glancing at my watch. "Dad might be home. Should we trade back?"

He shook his head. "Why? You're not doing anything wrong."

When we reached the top of the driveway, Dad was unloading tools from his truck. He glanced at us, then did a double take. We laughed, and I stopped too fast, leaving a patch in the gravel. I sat there a second, savoring my last seconds behind the wheel, while Uncle Gordo climbed out. Dad's face was frozen into a weird half grin, half frown.

"What's the matter, Mark, forgotten your long lost brother?" Uncle Gordo asked.

Dad tugged his mustache, the way he always does when he's nervous or embarrassed. Uncle Gordo held his arms open, but Dad just clapped him quickly on the shoulder. Uncle Gordo frowned, and there was an awkward second where no one seemed to know what to do or say. Finally Dad cleared his throat. "What a surprise," he said. "Does Blair know you're here?"

Uncle Gordo shook his head. "I don't think so. When no one answered your phone, I decided to come along. Hope you don't mind."

"Of course not," Dad said, but he didn't smile. I was confused. Why wasn't he happy to see Uncle Gordo? I climbed out of the car and waited for Dad to say hello to me, but his eyes were glued to the BMW. "New car, huh?" Dad asked.

Uncle Gordo nodded. "Bought it last week. Couldn't resist."

Dad frowned. "You must be raking it in at the restaurant."

My uncle laughed. "I wish. Actually, I got it cheap." He grinned at Dad. "You sound a little jealous."

Uncle Gordo was right; Dad looked like a kid who'd lost out on his share of the Halloween candy. "Hey, Dad," I said. "How was your week?"

He stared at me, startled. "Oh, hi, Todd. I was so surprised to see your uncle, I forgot to say hello." He gave me a quick, halfway hug. "How's soccer going?" he asked.

"Brutal," I said. "I could hardly walk the first few days."

Dad smiled. "If it's too terrible, you can always come to New Hampshire; do a little work for me before school starts."

"Forget it," I said. "I tried that already."

Uncle Gordo rolled his eyes at me. They were the same rust brown color as Dad's and mine. "Pretty bossy, was he?"

I laughed. "How'd you know?"

Uncle Gordo's mouth twitched. "Personal experience, you might say."

Dad looked him up and down. "Yeah, but it didn't last long. You finally got so big, I was no match for you anymore."

Uncle Gordo leaned against the BMW, resting his arm on the roof of the car. "Seems to me you've still got some pretty strong opinions about my life."

"Darned right," Dad said. "For example, what are you doing letting an inexperienced driver experiment with such a fancy automobile?"

I held my breath, but Uncle Gordo didn't even flinch. "Actually, Todd and I had a nice little spin together," he said. "He's good behind the wheel."

Dad nodded. "But fast," he said. "He drives like most teenagers—as if he's immortal."

I glared at Dad.

"Well, if you want to risk wrecking it, I guess it's your choice," Dad added, and went back to unloading his truck.

I crossed my arms over my chest. "Gee, *thanks,* Dad—"

Uncle Gordo put his hand on Dad's shoulder. "I didn't mean to make trouble," he said.

Dad sighed. "You never *mean* to. But you did. As usual."

I watched Dad's face, then my uncle's. Gordo made trouble? Since when?

Uncle Gordo raised his hand. "Let's not get into those old squabbles now. They're pretty boring, don't you think? Especially for Todd."

Dad opened his mouth, glanced at me, then took a deep breath. "Right," he said, and tried to smile. I felt uncomfortable. I'd never thought about Dad and Uncle Gordo having fights. Was this how Molly and I would be in thirty years?

I was about to take off when the door opened and Blair came out, squinting in the bright sunlight. "Gordon!"

she called, running to him. "I didn't hear you come."

They hugged each other and started chattering. Blair seemed happier to see my uncle than Dad was.

"Help me unload the truck, will you?" Dad asked, catching me by the arm. "It's been a long week."

"You can say that again," I said. We stowed his tools in the barn, neither one of us saying much. On the way to the house I asked, "Can I use the car tonight?"

Dad ran his fingers through his hair, which always looked as messy as mine; sawdust fluttered down onto his shoulders. "Not the Subaru—but the truck's all yours. I'd like to take Blair and your uncle to dinner."

I cleared my throat. "The thing is—well, I was hoping to ask Kai out." And the truck's not the most romantic vehicle in the world, I wanted to add, but I didn't. "Maybe you could ride with Uncle Gordo," I said as we climbed the steps. "Then I could use the Subaru."

Blair and my uncle were sitting on the porch swing, drinking lemonade. Uncle Gordo handed an extra glass to Dad. "Someone need a vehicle?" he asked.

Dad shook his head, gulping the lemonade down. "Thanks, but we're all set. Todd can take the truck." He glanced at Blair. "I thought we might go out for Italian food."

Uncle Gordo took a long drink of lemonade. "Want to come along?" he asked me. When I hesitated, he added quickly, "Sorry, I'm being stupid. It's Friday night, isn't it. Got a date?"

"Well—not exactly. At least—I haven't gotten around to calling her yet."

Uncle Gordo took off his glasses and rubbed them on his shirt. "Probably a lot nicer to take a girl out in a car then a truck full of greasy tools and nails."

Dad shot him an annoyed look, but Uncle Gordo ignored him.

"Tell you what," Uncle Gordo said. "We'll take my car and you can have the Subaru—or better yet," he told my parents, "let Todd drive the BMW. He handles it well."

Blair raised her eyebrows. "You've driven it?" she asked me.

When I nodded, her green eyes sparkled. "Lucky you," she said. "Do I get a turn tomorrow?"

Uncle Gordo opened his arms wide. "My car is your car," he said in a singsong voice.

But Dad wasn't smiling; in fact, I could tell he was just barely keeping his temper. "Gordon, that's a nice offer, but I don't want you to take that risk," he said. "Todd's only had his license a few months—"

"Six," I interrupted.

"Not long enough," he said.

Uncle Gordo smiled. "But, Mark, he's been driving your tractor and truck around this place since he was big enough to reach the pedals."

Dad leaned against the post, crossing his arms. "That's a little different than fooling around with a fancy automobile," he said.

For once I kept my mouth shut. Please, Uncle Gordo, say the right thing, I prayed silently. My uncle finished his lemonade, set it on the table and asked me, "Where were you planning to go tonight?"

I shrugged. "Not far. Maybe to the movies or something. Look, Uncle Gordo, it's no big deal. I can take the
truck—"

"Of course it's a big deal," Uncle Gordo interrupted.
"What kid your age wouldn't die for a chance to take his
friends out in a nice car?" He cocked one eyebrow. "What
if I asked you to limit your riders to one at a time—stick
to the back roads—and come home by eleven." He
glanced at Dad. "Sound all right to you, Mark?"

"Since when are you setting the rules for Todd?" Dad
snapped.

Uncle Gordo looked hurt. Blair stood up and put her
arm around my waist. It still surprised me, how much
shorter she was than me now. "I'm sure Todd will be
careful," she said. "Look at his eyes, Mark. Can't you see
how much fun it would be for him?"

Dad sighed. "Blair, that's hardly the point."

"Why not?" she said. "As long as Gordon doesn't
mind. After all, it's his car, so it's between him and
Todd." Blair reached up and ruffled Dad's hair. "You're
just jealous," she said. "If you're nice to your brother,
maybe he'll give you a ride tomorrow."

"Well—" Dad began, but that little second of hesita-
tion was enough for Uncle Gordo and me. He dug into
his pocket and flipped me the keys. "She's all yours. Just
don't do anything I wouldn't do."

"*That's* a good one!" Dad sputtered, laughing at last.

"Gee, thanks, Uncle Gordo," I said quickly. "I'll be
careful, I promise."

Dad started ranting about safety and driving slowly.

When he was done, I nodded, gave him a high five, and hurried inside to take a shower, gripping the keys. I wasn't about to turn down an offer that comes only once in a lifetime to a guy who's sixteen—and doesn't have a car of his own.

# Chapter Seven

A few hours after Uncle Gordo arrived, I was cruising down our road in his BMW, one arm resting on the open window, the warm air brushing my face, my hand gripping the steering wheel—and it wasn't a dream. It was so easy to pretend the car was mine. Uncle Gordo had even left me his Bob Marley tape. The deep reggae beat sang along with the hum of the tires.

"Sweet!" I called to the evening. The tall grass growing in the ditches flickered in the headlights; bugs spattered against the windshield. My right foot kept a steady pressure on the accelerator, begging me to push the pedal to the floor. But I restrained myself, remembering Dad's last words as I turned around in the driveway: "No speeding. Remember, this is a machine, not a toy. You're responsible for anything that goes wrong."

"Nothing will go wrong with *this* baby," I said now. I took it easy on the straightaway, then grabbed the wheel with both hands when I reached the tight corners before Kai's house. "Wait until Kai sees this," I said jacking the music up a notch. My plan was to wheel into the driveway, ask her to come outside, and then enjoy her amazed expression when she saw the car. Instead, I tore around the last curve (going a little too fast, I admit) and screeched to a halt. The Stewarts' driveway was filled with cars.

At first I thought Kai's parents were having people over, until I recognized Craig's beat-up Pontiac and a tan Chevy wagon with California plates that must be the Beekmans'. I pulled off the road and sat there a minute with my heart ticking as loud as the engine. A weird blue light flashed on and off behind the sliding glass doors of the Stewarts' family room; shadowy figures bounced in front of it, and the Spin Doctors blared from an open window.

Clearly, Kai was having a party. And clearly, I wasn't invited.

I tried to puzzle it out. Kai had seemed pretty friendly at the lake—so what was going on?

I restarted the engine, flicked on the headlights, and jammed the transmission into reverse. I was about to speed back down the driveway when the glass door slid open and Kai came out, followed by Rita, Trish, and Molly.

"Wouldn't you know," I muttered. "My own sister gets invited, but I don't." I forgot, conveniently, that Molly and Kai had been friends forever.

The girls huddled under the big pine tree a minute, trying to figure out who I was. Then Trish squealed, "Molly, it's your brother!" and they hurried over, surrounding the car, their mouths open. Even my sister looked stunned.

"Where'd you get this?" Molly demanded.

I shrugged. "Oh, it's a little something I picked up with my summer earnings."

"You expect me to believe that?" Molly scoffed.

"Just kidding," I said. "It's Uncle Gordo's. He let me borrow it tonight."

Molly's eyes lit up. "Uncle Gordo's here?"

I nodded. "For the weekend. Dad was all bent out of shape when Gordo let me have the car. I think he wanted a turn himself."

"Of course," Molly said. "When can I drive it?"

"Never," I said. "We don't want any crashes."

"Gee, thanks." She pulled up the hood of her sweat-shirt, pouting.

I glanced at Kai, who was leaning against the hood. "I was going to offer you a ride, Kai; I didn't realize you had *other* plans tonight."

Rita looked uncomfortable and edged away. I revved the engine but Trish put her hand on my arm. "Take us all for a drive, Todd—please?"

I shook my head. "My uncle said only one passenger at a time. He's pretty picky about the way I treat the car."

Trish cocked her head to the side and gave me her famous flirtatious smile. "I don't blame him."

"Yeah. Well, have fun tonight." I touched the accel-erator. Trish and Molly moved into the shadows with Rita, watching, but Kai grabbed the door and held on, running beside the car.

"Todd, don't be a jerk," she gasped. "Wait! I was going to call and ask you over—I promise."

I touched the brake and stopped slowly. "Let go," I said, trying to pry her fingers off the handle. "You'll get hurt."

Kai shook her head and gripped the door frame, her silver rings glinting against the chrome. "This wasn't planned," she insisted, breathing hard. "Mrs. Beekman gave me a ride home from the lake. Then Molly and Trish stopped by—and it turned into a party. We were just calling people when you came in. Right?" She turned around, but the other girls were out of earshot.

"Lighten up," Kai said. She leaned in the window until I felt her breath on my cheek. "You're so serious these days. We've only got one more week of vacation— don't spoil it."

The engine purred; I let it hum, leaving it in neutral. "I know there's only a week left," I said. "And I thought we'd spend some of it together."

"We will." Kai tugged my arm. "Come in and dance. I'll go for a ride with you later, after people leave. I promise."

"I have to have the car home by eleven," I said.

"No problem," she said. "Please, Todd?"

Her shiny black eyes met mine. "Oh, all right," I said, giving in. "Let me pull over."

She smiled, her teeth flashing. "Wait—I'll get in while you park." She jumped into the passenger's seat and I drove the car up near the house, finding a spot as far from other cars as possible. I didn't want any scratches.

"Nice, huh?" I asked, turning off the engine.

Kai nodded. "Your uncle must be a good guy."

"He is," I said. "He's cool." I put my arm around her.

Kai pulled away. "Don't," she said. "Everyone can see us."

"So what?" I asked, but she was already out of the car. I got out; I had no choice but to follow her inside.

A blue light flashed on and off from the corner of the room. I squinted, trying to see familiar faces in the blur of people who danced and sang along with the Spin Doctors' "Little Miss Can't Be Wrong." It was a funny mix of high school kids and Kai's friends from the theater. I picked out Rita, Alex, and Craig, then Molly and Trish, who swayed near the couch.

Kai yanked my hand. "Come on," she said, cupping her hand over my ear. "Dance with me."

"In a minute." To tell the truth, now that I saw how many people were here, I wondered if she'd lied about planning to call me. I went to the stereo and shuffled through the tapes, watching from the corner of my eye. Even my sister was on the floor now, pulling off her sweatshirt and letting her hair loose from its ponytail. Craig drew her into the circle everyone had made around Alex and Rita.

I stared. The twins were going nuts, undulating and stomping their feet as if they were the only ones on the floor. They slid gracefully across the oak boards, their movements compact, but rhythmic. Alex's eyes were half hidden by his hair, but Rita never took her eyes off her brother. When Alex shifted from side to side, she did too; when Alex twirled, Rita spun around in midair, ending up facing him again. Suddenly they went into a routine that was so smooth, I figured they must have practiced a thousand times. First Rita twirled under Alex's arm, then Alex let Rita spin him by the waist. Her hands wound him up like a top, then let him loose. Each twirl and twist was followed by another maneuver; they were like a pair of figure skaters, perfectly synchronized. The intense drum beat seemed to flow right through them.

I edged into the circle. Kai took my hand, dancing beside me, but I hardly noticed. I was mesmerized by the way the twins seemed to be inside each other's skulls; they moved like mirror images of one another. When the blue light flashed, Alex looked paler than ever, but Rita was flushed. Her hair swung to its own beat, the blue light flecking the strands with silver.

I danced harder now, feeling pumped up. Something was different about Alex. It took me a minute to figure it out: he was smiling, looking happy for the first time since I'd met him.

Trish wiggled past me, weaving through the twins. She took Craig's hand, then Molly's, pulling everyone closer together. Rita caught my eye and smiled, but she never lost the beat. When the final drum roll shook the speakers, Craig whistled and clapped the twins' shoulders. "Man, you two can sure dance. Is that what they taught in Hollywood?"

Alex smiled. "Holly*weird*, you mean. Yeah, we learned to dance in L.A., watching people on the boardwalk." When he caught me listening, his smile stiffened. "Hi, Todd. I didn't see you come in. How're you doing?"

"Fine." We pulled sodas from a bucket of ice near the couch; headlights swept across the driveway and Kai slipped through the sliding glass doors. I peered out the window, making sure the BMW was okay.

"See someone out there?" Craig asked.

"Just checking my car." I grabbed a handful of chips. "Nice party."

Craig nodded and took a long drink of soda. "Kai's got a great place. Too bad she doesn't stay here year round. Sad for you, too—what will you do when she goes back to Boston?"

"Who knows," I said.

Just then, doors slammed and a familiar voice rose from the shadows outside. "Oh, no—here comes trouble," Craig muttered, raising his eyebrows and nodding toward the glass doors. Tovitch and Dexter sauntered past, then stood in the pool of light outside the house. Tovitch carried a paper bag, which he shoved under Kai's chin, forcing her to look inside. She shook her head, then pointed toward the front of the house, probably warning him that her parents were home.

"Five dollars says there's beer in that sack," Craig said.

I nodded and glanced at Alex. His face was contorted, and his hands were clenched into tight fists.

"What do you say, guys," Craig asked. "Shall we ask them to take a hike?"

The girls, leaning against the back of the couch, stopped talking. Tovitch pulled a few cans from the bag. Without the music, the pop and sizzle of a beer-can opening seemed extra loud. Tovitch skimmed foam from the top, then took a deep swig.

"Well?" Craig asked.

My mouth felt dry as I thought about Tovitch falling into the lake; his threats as he floundered in the water. Luckily he hadn't seen me. "It's Kai's party," I said quietly.

"Yeah, but it's our soccer team," Alex said.

"He's right," Craig said. "Remember last year, when the coach heard some of the guys were drinking and the seniors had to sit out the next two games?"

"Of course. That's when the coach used me as a varsity sub. But Crawford won't know about Tovitch unless one of us turns him in," I said. "And I'm not about to do that. I'd rather stay alive."

Craig didn't answer; Alex shifted uncomfortably.

"So," Tovitch said in a loud voice, "whose fancy car? I almost rammed it."

I couldn't make out Kai's answer, but she must have said my name, because Randy's mouth opened wide, showing his chipped tooth, and he laughed, peering into the room. "Living high, O'Connor?" he called. He leered at Kai and let his hand glide down her back as if he owned her. Kai gave him a little shove and something hot erupted in my gut.

"Jerk!" I yelled, lunging for the door.

"Easy, man," Craig warned, grabbing my arm.

"A fight's just what he wants," Alex said, gripping my other elbow. "Kai can take care of it." I struggled to get away, and then a bunch of stuff happened at once: the lights flicked on overhead; Kai's dad called out, "Rita Beekman? You have a phone call—" and Tovitch, glancing inside, tossed his beer can into the bushes. That's when he saw me.

"Well, well. If it isn't my friend Todd," Tovitch said. "Too bad you can't come outside. I see you're busy with lover boy. We've got a score to settle, you know."

I tried to pull away from Alex and Craig, but it was too late. Tovitch and Dex melted into the shadows, and a second later I heard the throaty sound of Randy's truck starting up.

I was out the door in a second with my uncle's keys in my hand. Out of the corner of my eye I saw Randy's taillights swing to the left; he was headed toward town. I grabbed Kai and dragged her to the BMW, nearly shoving her into the passenger's seat.

"Hey!" she yelled. "What do you think you're doing?"

"What does it look like?" I asked. "Taking you for a ride. Watch out." She opened her mouth to protest, then clutched the dashboard as I slammed the door. I jumped in on the driver's side and started the engine, jamming it into reverse as I fumbled for the lights. "Put your seat belt on," I said, screeching down the driveway. I turned downhill, slowly goosing the accelerator. The sudden surge of the engine gave me a rush. I sat up straight, my eyes glued to the road.

"Cut it out!" Kai begged. "Slow down!"

"Don't worry," I said. "This baby handles like a dream." I accelerated into third, then fourth, watching the tachometer, my eyes peeled for Randy's taillights. He had a lead on me, but I knew the Beemer could catch him.

"Todd, stop; I want to get out!" Kai yelled, but I ignored her. The three hairpin turns were coming up. I downshifted and double-clutched, every muscle tense as the transmission whined from overdrive to fourth, then third. I struggled to keep the speed steady while the Beemer took the curves. She held the first one tight; I overcorrected, came into the second a little too wide, and was into the last one before I could catch my breath. I was panting and my hands were so sweaty, I could barely hold the wheel.

I might have made it, but when I came out of the third curve, going much too fast, Randy's truck was right in front of me, stopped dead in the middle of the road.

"Damn it!" I hit the brakes and swerved, just missing the pickup. We squealed down the left side of the road, heading straight for the woods, with Kai screaming her head off. I was too frightened to make a sound. I wrestled the car toward an opening in the tree line, feeling every bump and stone jar my body as we jolted past the ditch, hit a rock, and bumped along a farmer's access road into a field. We skidded across the stubble of mown hay and shuddered to a stop.

I cut the engine. My heart was hammering so loud, I thought my chest might split open. I stared straight ahead, then made myself look at Kai. Her face was dead white, and she'd wrapped her arms tight around her knees like someone getting ready for a plane crash. I put out my hand, but she slapped me.

"Don't touch me," she sobbed. "You're a complete and total *jerk*. I don't ever want to speak to you again."

I lowered my head to the steering wheel and closed my eyes while hot tears fell on my hands. Nothing but a miracle, I thought, could save me now.

# Chapter Eight

After what seemed like hours, we heard Tovitch and Dexter stumbling toward us in the dark, laughing rudely.

"Going a little too fast, O'Connor?" Randy taunted.

"Had to get away from lover boy, didn't you?" Dex said, setting his elbow on the Beemer's roof.

"Shut up," I said, gritting my teeth.

Suddenly Kai leaned across me, glaring at them. "Get out of here," she said, a sob catching in her throat. "Leave us alone."

Tovitch put up his hands. "Whatever you say. Just thought we could help." He stuck his ugly face in the window. His breath reeked of beer. "See what happens when you try to push me around? It's bad luck, O'Connor."

They disappeared. Kai huddled in her seat. "Take me home," she said, her voice quivering.

But I couldn't move, not yet. I sat still for another long minute, then slowly uncurled my fingers from the steering wheel and climbed out. I circled the Beemer, running my hands over her sleek sides, checking for dents. Nothing. I nearly sobbed out loud.

The real miracle was that the car actually started. A couple of pumps on the accelerator and it purred like an old cat.

I kept the Beemer in second all the way to Kai's house. She tapped her fingers on the dash and refused to look at me. That was bad enough, but I had worse things to worry about: Uncle Gordo, for instance.

By the time I pulled into Kai's driveway, my teeth were chattering as if had a fever, and my fingers jiggled so much, I dropped the keys on the floor and could hardly pick them up. I opened the window and leaned back in my seat, gulping air.

"What's wrong now?" Kai asked. Her voice came out of an iceberg.

"What's *wrong*? I'm screwed, that's what." I turned to stare at her. "Do you realize what my uncle will say when he finds out about this?"

"Your *uncle*?" Her eyes flashed. "Is that all you can think about? You could have killed us."

"Yeah, but I didn't." When she scowled at me, I said quickly, "I'm sorry, Kai; I *was* a jerk. Please don't be angry." I put my arm around her, but she shoved me aside. She was crying again.

"You're *both* jerks," she said. "You and Randy. You push me around like you own me or something." Kai climbed out of the car. "Next time you need to puff yourself up in front of him, leave me out. I'd like to stay alive for a few more years."

She slammed the door so hard I thought the glass would break. "Kai!" I yelled. "Wait!"

She stalked toward the house like some proud bird, her head held high and her back straight. Would she tell her parents—or play it cool?

All of a sudden the thought of dealing with *my* parents—not to mention Uncle Gordo—brought my dinner into my throat. I lunged from the car and hit the bushes just in time. Then I lay on the ground, shivering, until I found the energy to stumble back to the Beemer. I climbed in on the passenger's side and clenched my teeth, but they kept right on chattering.

"Todd, what happened? Kai said you were in big trouble."

I opened my eyes. Molly was staring at me through the open window, her face puckered. "What did you do to Kai? She says she never wants to see you again."

I groaned. "Oh, yeah? Well, I had a little accident," I said. "You'll have to drive me home."

Molly held onto the door. "But, Todd, I'm only allowed to drive with someone over twenty-one—"

"So pretend I'm older," I said. "It's an emergency. Please. It's only three miles."

"Should we go to the doctor?" she said.

"No, I'm just shook up. I lost my dinner in the bushes. Come on, let's split before people start asking questions."

Molly drove like a complete beginner at first, gripping the wheel as if it were her first day in driver's ed. Every time she shifted, the poor Beemer jerked, coughed, and sent nasty signals to my stomach. But by the time we hit our road, Molly was getting the hang of it; she even had a smile on her face. I couldn't relax; my eyes were glued to the side mirror, praying I wouldn't see the Subaru behind us. Luckily we crossed the bridge and climbed the driveway without passing a single car.

"Pull up under the light, near the barn," I said, "and jump out quick in case they drive in."

After she turned the engine off, I checked the car more carefully and found a deep scratch on the driver's door. "Ouch," I whispered, running my finger along the ugly gouge. Then I got a flashlight from the truck and lay on my back beside the Beemer. It was too dark to be certain, but she looked all right underneath. I opened the hood and stared at the engine, but I didn't know enough to tell if anything was wrong.

Molly was leaning against the door frame of the barn with her hood pulled tight around her face, even though it was still warm out. "So what happened?" she asked.

"I was going too fast on the curves." As I described my near miss with Randy's truck, the way I lost control right afterward, I felt like I was viewing an instant replay complete with vivid details: Kai's mouth frozen open in a scream; the rough bark of a maple tree so close, as the car hurtled past, I was sure it would tear off the door; the coarse stubble of the hay field.

When I opened my eyes, Molly stood beside me, our shoulders just touching. "You all right?" she asked.

I nodded, but leaned against her, grateful for the support. "What am I going to tell him?"

"Who, Uncle Gordo? The truth, what else?" Molly's

gray eyes were steady and clear. Things like that always came easy to her, for some reason.

"Yeah," I said, looking away. "I was kind of hoping I wouldn't have to say anything."

Molly stuck her hands into her sweatshirt pockets. "He'll notice the scratch, and there might be something else wrong. Besides, he was pretty wild when he was a kid."

"That doesn't mean he'll understand." There were plenty of family stories about Uncle Gordo's escapades as a teenager. But he'd trusted me, and I'd blown it. My face crumpled. "God, Mol, I came so close to crashing. I could have wrecked the car, hurt Kai—no wonder she hates me."

"She'll get over it." Molly gave me a quick hug, patting my back gently, then handed me a piece of paper towel from the truck to wipe my face. When we heard the sound of an engine at the foot of the hill, we both froze. "They're home," Molly said in a rush. She ran into the barn and snapped off the light. "Here, make a run for it," she said, shoving the car keys into my hand. Headlights swept across the bridge. "I'll keep them away from the car somehow; tell them you've gone to bed. When it's safe to talk to Gordo, I'll come get you. Hurry."

I ran for the porch without looking back, hurtled through the kitchen, and took the back stairs two at a time. I shut my door and flung myself across my bed, breathing hard, lying there for ages while Blair and Dad talked in the kitchen. I heard Uncle Gordo greet Molly with a yell outside; they stood under my window and chatted about the party for a minute. Molly told him about the dancing, but she was cool; she didn't squeal on me. Crisco whined at the kitchen door, then glasses clinked and water ran in the sink. Wouldn't they ever go to bed?

I must have dozed off, because next thing I knew, the hall light swept across my face. I jerked awake and sat up quickly. Molly stood beside me in her nightgown. "All clear," she whispered. "Uncle Gordo's still making noise in the den. Blair and Dad's light is off."

I groaned softly. My mouth tasted as if I'd been chewing on an old sweater. "Thanks for covering for me," I whispered.

She raised her hand. "No problem." In a few seconds her door clicked shut at the end of the hall.

Come on, kiddo, get it over with, I told myself. I took off my shoes, tiptoed downstairs, and stood outside the den for a second, holding my breath and praying Uncle Gordo was asleep. But there was a bar of light under the door, and I heard a thump, then a squeak; he was probably fixing up the sofa bed. "Uncle Gordo?" I called softly.

"Come in," he answered.

I opened the door. Uncle Gordo padded around the bed in his bare feet, pulling a sheet over the mattress. He wore a pair of loose gray sweats and a faded T-shirt. With his glasses off he looked sleepy and rumpled, like an old bear.

"Have fun?" he asked, then squinted. "Say, you're a little green around the gills."

"Yeah, I lost my dinner. Among other things." I held out the car keys; they clinked together, shaking along with my hand. "Uncle Gordo—" I took a deep breath. "I screwed up your car."

His face hardened. "What do you mean."

"I went off the road. No one was hurt—" I gulped, not knowing how to start. Uncle Gordo shut the door and pointed at the open sofa. "Have a seat." He pulled out the desk chair and sat astride it with his arm across the back, facing me. "Well?"

I took a deep breath. "There's this kid, Randy Tovitch; he's on the soccer team. A good player, but a jerk. We had a run-in at the lake today—I pushed him in; now he's mad. So tonight at Kai's—she's my girl, or at least, she *was*—he made a move for her, and I lost it."

I stopped. It sure sounded stupid the way I was describing it.

"Go on," Uncle Gordo said quietly.

I did, speaking slowly, telling how I'd chased Randy down the road, taken the curves too fast. When I got to the part about the trees and the opening into the field, Uncle Gordo winced and shook his head sadly.

"Kai was in the car with you?"

"Yeah. That was dumb. I was showing off, just like she said."

He rested his head on his folded arms and stayed quiet for a long time. "Anything else?" he asked at last.

"Not really. The car started all right; I took Kai home, blew lunch, and made Molly drive me here."

A tiny smile tugged at Uncle Gordo's mouth. "What

a sneak—Molly never mentioned that she'd been behind the wheel of my machine. She's covering for you nicely, eh?"

I nodded. "Yeah." My voice cracked. "I'm really sorry. There's a bad scratch on the door—I hope nothing else is wrong." I brushed away the tears with the back of my hand. "We should have listened to Dad. I was an idiot. I lost it completely."

He nodded, pushing his long hair off his face. "Sure sounds like it. Thank God no one was hurt; I'd never forgive myself."

This made me feel even worse. I'd never thought about what it would be like for my uncle if something awful had happened. He stood up, took his glasses from the desk, and wiped them on his shirt, then padded back and forth at the end of the room. Why didn't he say anything? I wondered if he was like Dad: silent before he exploded.

"I'll pay for fixing the scratch," I said quickly, "and anything else that's wrong. I earned plenty of money at the lumberyard this summer."

He put up his hand. "Don't worry about that now. We'll discuss it in the morning." He sat on the other side of the bed and studied me until I had to look away.

"If your parents knew about this, what would they do?" he asked.

I leaned against the back of the sofa. This wasn't going to be easy after all. "I'd be nailed. Dad would never forgive me—" I picked at the sheet with my fingernails. "You think I have to tell them?"

Uncle Gordo hesitated. "That's up to you. I don't want

to rat on you or give my brother something else to gloat about." I was surprised by how bitter he sounded, but I didn't dare interrupt. He held my fate in his big calloused hands, resting on his knees.

"After they were done yelling at you, what would your punishment be?" he asked.

I sat back up. "They'd take away my car privileges."

Uncle Gordo ran his fingers through his hair, parting the tangles. "Maybe you should ground yourself for a while. Do some jobs around the place—and think about what might have happened."

"I'm doing that already." Which was true. All the time he was talking, someone cruel was playing back the movie inside my head, showing me those last few minutes before we left the road. I tried to concentrate on Uncle Gordo's bristled cheeks and sad eyes so Randy's truck would stop appearing in front of me like a huge blue wall.

I started to get up, but Uncle Gordo put a hand on my shoulder. "Hold on," he said. "Let's get back to the reason this happened. The kid who's bugging you— what's going on between you and him?"

I drew back, startled; Tovitch seemed beside the point right now. But Uncle Gordo obviously wanted an answer. "Tovitch is a pain in the butt," I told him. "He's after my girl—among other things."

Uncle Gordo pulled his T-shirt over his stomach and cocked his head at me. "I can't imagine you'd have too much trouble handling that," he said.

I shifted uneasily on the bed. "It's actually kind of complicated," I said. "He's always throwing insults around. I forgot to ignore them, that's all; I overreacted."

Uncle Gordo stood up. "And when you caught up to him, what were you planning to do? Run him off the road?"

My right leg bounced up and down and my throat felt dry. "I don't know," I admitted. "I guess—I hadn't really thought about it."

He nodded. "That's the trouble with people like you and me—we don't think, until it's too late." He went to the window and stood there for a minute with his back to me, staring into the dark. "For years I'd fly off the handle first, think later. Never got me anywhere except into hot water." He sighed. "I wish it hadn't taken me this long to learn how to think first, then act."

Sweat trickled from my forehead. I felt pretty woozy, to tell the truth. "Uncle Gordo, I'm really sorry," I said. "I didn't mean to treat your car that way—you were cool, to let me drive it—"

He turned around, putting both hands up in front of his chest. "Enough," he said. "We both made mistakes tonight." I guess he thought loaning me the car wasn't such a hot idea after all. I leaned against the pillows and clenched my teeth, ordering my stomach to stay quiet, wishing the room would stop whirling.

Uncle Gordo hoisted me up by my shoulders and kept his arm around me until I was standing straight. "Okay, Todd?"

I nodded. "We'll check the car over in the morning," Uncle Gordo said. "If it looks bad, maybe you can advance me a little cash."

"Sure," I said, blinking. My eyes were getting heavy.

Uncle Gordo maneuvered me toward the door and paused with his hand on the latch. "If you can't work things out with this Tovitch kid, give me a call. Sometimes it helps to talk with someone outside the situation."

"Okay. Thanks." We said good night, and I stumbled upstairs, undressed, and sank down on my mattress, expecting to fall asleep instantly.

But it didn't work. Every time I started to drift off, I saw the tree trunks jumping together, vibrating like knives thrown from the sky. I tossed and turned until I was completely tangled in the sheets, then reached for my headset. I put in a Muddy Waters tape, adjusted the volume, and lay down with my head at the wrong end of the bed, watching the moonlight creep through the branches of the maple tree. But even the bluesy guitar chords couldn't erase the squeal of brakes or the sound of Kai's scream ringing in my ears.

# Chapter Nine

Grounding myself turned out to be a whole lot easier than being punished by my parents. I decided to stay home all weekend, then drive the car only to practice and back during the week. My parents were surprised, especially when they got up Saturday morning and discovered I'd already waxed and polished the BMW. I was protecting myself, of course; the wax hid the scratch a bit and I wanted to check out the car in the daylight. As far as I could see, there wasn't anything else the matter.

Dad's eyebrows zoomed up when he found me next to the barn with the bucket and sponge. "Wish you'd do that to the Subaru," he said, so I did, which shocked him even more. Then I spent the afternoon with him and Molly in the family room, taping the new plasterboard. I could tell my sister was itching to know more details, but she kept her mouth shut as long as our parents were around.

"You're not going out, Todd?" Blair asked when she heard I'd be home for dinner.

I shook my head. "No, I want to see Uncle Gordo."

Which was true. Plus, the thought of being behind the wheel of a car, even a junker like the Subaru, made my stomach turn over again.

Sometime in the late afternoon, when Uncle Gordo was taking a walk, Molly finally got me alone outside. "What did he say?" she asked.

"He was pretty decent, considering." I kept my voice low. "He suggested that I ground myself for the weekend; I won't drive much during the week, either."

She grinned. "You're just lucky he didn't tell Dad."

"He didn't want to," I said. "It was weird—"

"Careful," Molly said softly. Dad came out of the barn, carrying another bucket of spackling compound. We waited until he went past. "What about Kai?" Molly asked.

I kicked the gravel with the heel of my sneaker, gouging out a hole. "Who knows. If she doesn't want to talk to me—"

"You could call her," Molly suggested.

"Right. And listen while she slams down the phone."

"Maybe if you apologize—"

"I did. Look, Mol, I know she's your best friend, but just stay out of it, okay?"

Molly's eyes narrowed. "So that's the thanks I get for covering for you?" She turned her back on me and stomped into the house. I flopped down in the grass and lay there a long time, watching a cloud inch toward the barn. I could only handle one angry girl at a time.

At the end of the day, Uncle Gordo and Blair picked vegetables in the garden, then spent an hour chopping them and making sauces for a stir-fry. When we sat down to eat, Uncle Gordo and Dad seemed friendlier. They got all cranked up telling stories about when they were kids.

"When your dad was Molly's age," Uncle Gordo told us, "too young for a license, he took the car to town. Thought he was so slick, until he locked the keys in the car and had to call home to get rescued." Uncle Gordo laughed. "I thought our father would have a heart attack. Mark was grounded for days."

"Weeks," Dad groaned.

I kept my eyes on my plate; so did Molly. This conversation was too close to home. Uncle Gordo nudged me. "See the fine example your father set for me? It's no wonder I was in trouble all the time."

Dad snorted. "Don't blame your problems on me. Especially the ones that lasted."

Uncle Gordo winced and pushed his vegetables around. I glanced at Molly, but she was playing it cool, looking across the table and out the window. Finally Blair changed the subject, and the nastiness passed.

When I woke up late on Sunday, Uncle Gordo was already gone, but he'd left a note under my door. "Don't worry about a thing," he wrote. "I'll call you as soon as I know what's up. Take care of the Randy situation. I'm sure you know what to do, but if not, the lines are open." It was signed with a big, splashy *G*.

After breakfast Blair, Dad, and Molly went canoeing. They invited me to come too, but I begged off. "I need to rest," I said. Which was only partly true. In fact, I was hoping to hear from Kai, and I waited all morning for her to call, but of course she didn't. Finally I switched on the answering machine, grabbed my soccer ball, and went outside to juggle. When I came in, the light was blinking on the tape. I switched it on, my heart racing.

"Yes," said a cold, steely voice. "This is Felicity Stewart. Mark, could you please call me when you come in?"

Damn. Kai's mom, sounding *very* pissed off, and she never called Dad; *not* a good sign. How would I deal with that one? I erased the tape fast and stood there a minute, foot tapping. Tomorrow was Monday. Dad would be in New Hampshire and Blair never answered the phone when she was in the darkroom. If Molly helped, I could get lucky. Maybe.

The phone jangled again by my ear, making me jump. I licked my lips. Should I pick it up? I finally answered on the fifth ring.

"Todd!" Coach Crawford's voice was gruff and businesslike. "Welcome to varsity soccer."

"Thanks. Thanks a lot."

"See you tomorrow at eight thirty sharp." That was it; he hung up without saying good-bye. My breath let out in a slow rush. Even though I'd been expecting it, I was glad to hear good news for a change.

When everyone came home in the late afternoon, Blair asked, "Any calls?"

I was prepared. "Not for you," I told her, which was true; Mrs. Stewart had asked for Dad. "Just one from the coach, telling me I made varsity."

Everyone fussed over me, which made me feel weird. Dad and Blair insisted on going to town for pizza (who could refuse?); I just made sure I was the last one out of the house, turning the tape machine off before closing the door. After dinner Dad left for New Hampshire and the phone stayed quiet. I was safe for one more day.

Monday morning I begged Molly to intercept calls and went off to practice full of resolutions: to drive slowly, fix things with Kai, and ignore Tovitch—somehow.

I did fine with my first promise; in fact, I was so slow going down our road that Mrs. Beekman, driving behind me with the twins, nearly went crazy. She hugged my bumper all the way to town while giant dust plumes trailed behind us.

I parked beside the fence and ducked my head as the twins went past, digging my cleats out from under the mess of bakery bags and dirty T-shirts on the floor. When I sat up, Mrs. Beekman was walking toward me across the parking lot. What could she want? I hadn't even met her yet. If I'd been polite, I would have climbed out, but I didn't want her to see I was driving barefoot. I thought of the rides I'd given the twins so far and licked my lips. Had she heard about the accident?

She leaned toward the car. "You must be Todd," she said. "I'm Sharon Beekman, Rita and Alex's mother."

"Hi," I said. "Nice to meet you." I shook her hand through the open window. You'd know she was from somewhere else from the way her glossy eye shadow matched her bright blue blouse. Her hair was blond, like Rita's, but it looked dyed. I shifted in my seat, dreading what she might say, but she surprised me by being really friendly.

"You were so kind to bring the twins home the other day," Mrs. Beekman said in a breathy voice. "I was wondering if you could give them a ride today; maybe tomorrow, too." She smiled, waiting. When I didn't answer, she added, "I have some job interviews, and I don't know if I'll be back in time to pick them up."

"A ride?" I hesitated, my brain scrambling for a quick excuse, but I couldn't find one. "Sure, no problem." Just the world's *biggest* problem, I wanted to say, but I kept a stiff smile on my face.

Mrs. Beekman opened her pocketbook. "Let me reimburse you for the gas."

I shook my head, even though I could sure use the cash after messing up the Beemer. "That's all right. I go that way anyhow. Really."

"Well, that's very nice of you, Todd. Thanks." She gave me a sad smile, and for a second she looked a little like Alex. "As soon as my husband arrives, we'll have another car, and the twins will be able to drive themselves around. We rented our house sight unseen, and we didn't realize how far it was from town."

I didn't know what to say, but it didn't matter; Mrs. Beekman kept right on talking.

"I really appreciate your being friendly to the twins," she said. "Alex went through some hard times in L.A. His dad and I hope it will be easier for him, living here."

What did *that* mean? I felt a strange prickling at the base of my neck.

"Well, thanks again," she said without explaining, and took off.

So Alex had troubles in L.A. Like the ones he was

having now? I pulled on my socks and cleats. Why did I say yes to that woman? Since Kai wasn't speaking to me anymore, giving Rita a ride wasn't a big deal. But having Alex in my car was another story.

I grabbed my ball, slammed the door, and started toward the field. It was early, so I hung out down by the goal box, juggling. I jumped when a familiar voice croaked, "Hey, how's our fag man this morning?"

Tovitch brushed by, jabbing me in the ribs, and kept right on going.

"What the—"

He glanced at me over his shoulder. " '*Really* appreciate your being friendly to the *twins*,' " he simpered, imitating Mrs. Beekman. " 'That's all right,' " he went on, scraping and bowing. " 'I go that way anyhow.' "

He'd been listening all that time? My shoulders tensed but I forced myself to smile. "Yeah, it's a drag—I couldn't think of an excuse fast enough."

Tovitch smirked. "I'll bet. Guess she hasn't heard what a great driver you are."

"Luckily," I said, juggling faster. I glanced at Tovitch, trying to read his mood. I wasn't sure where we stood after Friday. "Of course, I'm not used to finding trucks parked in the middle of the road."

Tovitch laughed. "I was taking a leak. I didn't expect you'd follow me at ninety miles an hour."

"Yeah," I said. "Stupid, huh?" I let the ball drop. "Listen, I'm sorry about pushing you into the lake—I couldn't resist."

I reached out to clap his shoulder, and Tovitch jerked backward, holding up his hands. "Don't *touch* me." He wiped his arm as if I'd spit on it. "I saw the way Beekman cozied up to you." His voice cracked. "I'm surprised you didn't take *Alex* on your joyride. No wonder Kai's had it. No girl wants to date a fag . . ."

I froze, my hand in the air. "What do you mean? You talked to her?"

A slow smile spread across his face. "Hey, I warned you. That was a nice bag of weed I lost—"

Something buzzed in my ears, and for a second I saw red. Literally. The soccer field, the kids kicking balls around, even the sky turned a vivid scarlet; the world was crimson. I charged Tovitch as if I were being sucked into a pool of molten lava, pummeling his arms, his face, whatever got in my way, hardly noticing when he punched me back. In an instant we were surrounded.

"O'Connor, lay off!"

"Fight! Fight!"

"Come on, Tovitch, nail him!"

"That's it, Todd, show him!"

"Todd! Randy! Break it up!"

I felt the hard crunch of muscle and bone beneath my knuckles. "Todd, lay off!" the coach roared, grabbing me from behind. My T-shirt tore. I staggered backward, and Tovitch stumbled to his knees, clutching his stomach. I wiped my arm across my face; blood streamed from my nose. Crawford helped Tovitch up, waving at the circle of guys who crowded around us.

"Beat it," Crawford said, sending everyone away. "Jog down to the river and back, all of you. Ozzie, make sure there's no cheating on the hill."

Tovitch slumped on the bench, and I couldn't move.

"Nice way to begin your varsity season, O'Connor," Crawford said. I kept my head down. Would he kick me off the team?

"What was *that* about?" the coach demanded.

I glanced at Tovitch. His upper lip was puffy and raw and his black eyes glowered at me from under his hair. He didn't say anything, but I read his warning loud and clear: *Keep your trap shut if you know what's good for you.*

"Nothing," I mumbled, spitting blood.

"A misunderstanding," Tovitch muttered.

Crawford jabbed me in the chest. " '*Nothing,*' " he mocked. "If 'nothing' makes you guys start a free-for-all, what happens when someone challenges you in a game? Huh? The last thing I need is two of my best players red-carded."

I almost smiled. Crawford thought of me as one of his best players? Then I bit my lip. At this rate I might not make it to a game.

"Sorry," I said quickly. I wiped my face on my T-shirt; it came away sticky with blood.

"Yeah," Tovitch said. "Didn't mean it."

Crawford sighed. "This is getting us nowhere." He crossed his arms and paced up and down. "You guys are entitled to your differences; I don't know what they are. Look at me, both of you!"

We did. Crawford's blue eyes glittered like pond ice in January, and his voice came out in a cold, slow hiss. "Those differences stay at home. There is no room for fighting on this team. No. Room. Understand?"

"Yes, sir," I said. Crawford paced between us, his muscular arms swinging dangerously each time he turned around. His eyes darted from Tovitch to me. "If you can work with the team, fine. If you can't, you're out of here. Simple as that." He glared at me, and I looked away; his gaze was too fierce to meet. "I'm surprised at you, O'Connor," he added. "I didn't think you went in for this sort of thing."

"I don't," I said quickly. Tovitch leered at me behind the coach's back. Crawford surprised us both by wheeling on him and gripping his shoulders with both hands.

"And you. After all I did to get you here—this is the thanks I get?" Tovitch blinked hard. The coach's voice dropped and I didn't know if he meant for me to hear, but I didn't dare move. "Soccer's your ticket out of here, Tovitch," Crawford said. "Don't screw up now. You hear me?"

"Yeah." Tovitch looked embarrassed, and I turned away. Craig was right; Tovitch was the coach's special pet.

Crawford eased up on Randy's shoulders with a sigh. "I should bench you guys for the rest of the week."

I found my voice. "Please don't, Coach," I begged. "This is it, I promise. No more fights."

He studied me, then looked at Tovitch, waiting.

"Right," Tovitch said, avoiding my face. "We're done."

Crawford stood beside the bench a minute, then said, "Okay—this is how it works. You're off the field the rest of this practice. Watch how the team looks with the two of you sitting here." He kicked the bench with the side of his foot. "You're our ball boys the rest of this week, and our clean-up crew, too."

"What about the first game?" I asked softly.

"We'll see. Right now, you're on probation. You can practice with us tomorrow, but I'll be watching your attitude," Crawford said. "I'd hate to start the season without you, but I will, if necessary. That means you too, Tovitch."

Randy's eyes widened, but he didn't make a sound. "Clean yourselves up," Crawford said. "And run some laps around the field. I want to see your blood pump." He took off.

*My* blood was pumping already; trickling down the back of my throat. I drew a cup of water from the big thermos and splashed it over my face, then bunched up my shirt and held it to my nose, trying to stop the bleeding.

"You won't get away with this, asshole," Tovitch warned me. "You're the one who started this fight."

I was careful not to answer. I tossed the cup on the ground and jogged down the field, refusing to look at him.


Tovitch and I avoided each other the rest of practice, and everyone else made wide circles around us. Over the weekend Crawford had picked a total squad of eighteen guys, including Tovitch and me. With the two of us on the bench and another two as keepers in the goals, the coach was playing seven against seven; three on each front line, two at midfield, two at fullback. Drew was at

left wing and Alex at striker, which of course had Tovitch
making nasty comments under his breath.

While the guys practiced, I ran lines, catching the ball
when it went out, tossing it back to the defensive man for
the throw-in. I wanted Crawford to see I was making an
effort. Plus, doing something useful made it easier to be
outside the game.

I kept my eye on Beekman. He made it look easy, as
always. His footwork was amazing, and you could tell by
the way his forehead puckered that he thought about
every move ahead of time. When he didn't have the ball,
he almost bounced to keep up with the play, tossing his
hair out of his eyes.

"Beekman, use the wing!" the coach called, and Alex
did, sending the ball along the line to Drew, who drilled
it into the goal just past Ozzie's outstretched fingers.

"Nice work! Way to pass!" Crawford yelled. "Let's see
more of that." I sighed. The coach was right; these guys
were doing fine without Tovitch or me—and they didn't
even have a full team on either side.

Crawford pulled everyone together before we went
home. Tovitch and I sat on opposite sides of the circle.
"Listen up," the coach said. "You're starting to play better as individuals, but I need to see more teamwork.
Talk to each other out there." He glanced at me, then
found Tovitch with his eyes. "This sport isn't about in-
dividual stars, it's about playing together. When you set
foot on the field, the team comes first. Got that?"

The guys murmured yes, and some of them glared at
Tovitch and me. I picked at the grass. "See you tomor-

row," Crawford said, and left us sitting on the ground.

The varsity girls went past, dragging their sweatshirts. I jumped up to collect a ball that had sailed over the fence at the far end of the field. I didn't want anyone—especially Rita—to see my bloody face. Tovitch left, conveniently forgetting to help me clean up, but that was fine with me; it was easier to do the job without him. While the team wandered off to the locker room, I tied up the net bag and sat down with Craig, who was unwinding an ace bandage from his ankle.

"Brutal," I said, expecting a smile, but Craig's dark eyes flashed at me.

"You and Tovitch could wreck the team," he said. "First the car chase, now the fight—what's going on?"

"You heard about my accident?"

Craig rubbed his ankle. "Sure. Tovitch is telling everyone."

I groaned. "If my parents hear, I'll be grounded forever. That idiot. What's he got against me?"

Craig inched closer, keeping his voice low. "It's not you, it's Beekman. Ever since Alex showed up, Randy has been impossible. He can't stand the fact that Alex is such a good player, especially since Beekman keeps ending up in the striker position. I'm sure that's why Tovitch has the backfield calling Alex a fag."

"Really?" I asked, playing dumb. "Since when?"

Craig put on his shoes. "Since about two minutes after Alex showed up. Come on, Todd, you know what's happening." When I didn't answer, Craig added, "How long do you think Beekman can take it?"

"You mean he might quit?"

"Wouldn't you, if you were new in town and all the guys called you names?" Craig's face was stormy, which surprised me; he'd always seemed easygoing, the kind of guy who gets along with everyone.

"I guess." I rubbed my nose, which wouldn't quit throbbing, and glanced around to make sure no one was listening. "What *about* Alex. Do you think he is a fag?"

Craig stared at me, then scrambled to his feet. "What if he is? I don't give a damn, and you shouldn't either." His voice was so cold, it scared me. "Calling Alex a fag might be like calling me nigger." He spat the words out, like he'd caught something foul in his mouth. "It doesn't matter which insult you use, it's still hate." He glared at me. "You've got a job ahead of you, O'Connor."

"Oh, yeah?" I said, trying to stay cool.

Craig pointed to the chain-link fence behind the bleachers, separating the field from the parking lot. "See that fence there? You think you can sit on it, not taking sides, hoping if you don't take a stand, everything will work out fine." He clenched his fists. "But it doesn't work that way. There's no place in the middle." He squatted on his heels so his eyes were level with mine. "A couple of guys aren't poisoned against Alex yet. Drew's all right; so's Ozzie. I thought you were with us." He sighed. "Guess I was wrong." He picked up his cleats, shoved his feet into his sandals, and stalked off, leaving me alone on the field.

# Chapter Ten

I waited until I thought everyone had left, then heaved myself to my feet and stumbled past the bleachers.

"Hey, Todd." Alex slipped out from the shadows, making me jump.

"Damn, you surprised me," I said, wondering if he'd heard my conversation with Craig.

"Are you all right?" Alex asked.

"Yeah—just a bloody nose. Nothing serious."

Alex stepped in front of me. "Did that fight have anything to do with me?"

"Not really," I lied, avoiding his eyes. "Randy's been on my case, that's all."

"Join the club," Alex said, and followed me to the parking lot. I was about to jump into my car and leave him behind when I remembered my promise to his mother. As if my life wasn't difficult enough, Rita was leaning against my car, surrounded by a bunch of girls. When she saw me, her smile disappeared. The girls stopped talking and stared at me.

"Todd!" Trish cried. "Your face!"

I popped open the back of the Subaru, found an old rag, and soaked it with water from my water bottle. I tried to clean up before the girls asked more questions. But it was hopeless. Trish sidled over and asked, "What happened?"

"I had a little fight this morning," I said, pulling on my sweatshirt. "And if you don't mind, I'd rather not talk about it."

Trish opened her eyes wide. "A fight? Really?"

"Afraid so." I tossed my ball and cleats into the car. I had to get out of there before she pried the whole story out of me. "Ready to go, Rita?" I blurted.

She seemed confused. "You're giving us a ride? I wasn't sure if my mother talked to you—"

"Yup, she did. Guess she hasn't heard about my excellent driving skills. Hop in. I promise to drive nice and slow." I yanked my door open. The twins hesitated, then climbed in.

"Rita, call me later," Trish cried as I pulled out of the parking lot.

The drive through town seemed endless. I kept my eyes glued to the road and the radio off, even though the silence nearly drove me nuts. My whole face was on fire, but I wasn't ready to check it out in the mirror. We went through the last traffic light, passed the theater, and headed out of town. For the first time since I'd met her, Rita didn't say a word, and I couldn't tell what Alex was thinking; his dark glasses reflected the inside of the car.

When we reached the junction of my road with Soldier's Hill, a familiar blue truck crested the hill above us and came barreling in our direction. I slammed on the brakes and swerved to the right, turning down my road before Tovitch got anywhere near us. I caught a glimpse of his dust plume in my rearview mirror. The Subaru rattled and shook until I slowed down.

"Sorry about that quick turn," I said, scrambling for an excuse. "My face is killing me; I'd like to go home and clean up. Do you mind coming to my house a minute?"

"Of course not." Rita finally looked at me. "Must be painful." She put her hand on the door handle. "Why don't you just let us off here; we can walk—"

"That's okay," I said. "I'll take you home later."

She shifted on the seat. "All right with you, Alex?" Rita sounded as if she wished he'd say no, but her brother didn't move. He sat frozen like a prisoner in the back of a police cruiser.

I turned into our driveway. When I crossed the bridge, Rita leaned forward, gripping the dashboard. "Look at all the sheep!" she exclaimed. I parked the car; Crisco limped over to meet us. Rita opened her door, bending to scratch the collie's ears.

"What a sweet old dog," she said. "What's her name?"

"Crisco," I told her. "She's ancient." Alex climbed stiffly out of the car, lagging behind as we walked to the house. I pointed to the porch swing. "Have a seat," I said. "I'll be right out. Want some lemonade?"

"Sure," Rita said. "I'll help you." She followed me inside. Alex scooped up my practice ball and juggled near the porch, the leather smacking his skin like a drumbeat.

I went straight to the sink and stuck my head under the faucet, letting the cold water run over my face. When

I came up for air, Rita stood beside me holding a clean dish towel. "Here," she said, "let me dry you off—I'll be careful."

She dabbed the towel gently over my face. It was heaven, feeling her fingertips brush my cheeks, even though my skin was bruised and sore. "I must look pretty bad," I said.

She shook her head. "No—just a little swollen." Her eyes met mine for a second; they looked sad.

"Thanks a lot." I went to the cupboard, took two aspirin, then finally worked up my nerve to check my face in the mudroom mirror. My nose was swollen and my freckles were blotchy, but it was nothing permanent. I couldn't help grinning, thinking that Randy would have a fat lip by now and no one to offer him sympathy. Served him right.

"You fought with Randy, didn't you?" Rita asked, spooking me. Could she read *my* mind, too?

I sighed. "Yeah." I hesitated. "He's still mad I shoved him into the lake on Friday."

Rita looked puzzled, but she didn't say anything else. I got out some ice and a tray; Rita filled the glasses, and we carried the lemonade to the porch. Alex dropped the ball, took a glass, and leaned against the railing. Rita sat beside me on the swing. We were all quiet, but it wasn't a comfortable kind of silence. Finally Rita finished her drink and set the glass down. "Maybe we should go home."

Alex crunched his last piece of ice. "In a minute." He took off his dark glasses and stared at me; gray circles rimmed his eyes. "Let's cut the bull," he said.

I set my heel against the floor, stopping the swing. My hands started to sweat. "What do you mean?" I asked.

"You lied. You only brought us here so Tovitch wouldn't see us in your car."

I ducked my head. "Randy knew I was bringing you home. He heard your mother talking to me."

"I see." Alex sat on the railing, his long legs stretched out in front of him. He tossed his hair back. "So why'd you avoid him?"

Rita sat still with her hands between her knees, her eyes fixed on my face. I stood up fast, nearly knocking her off the swing. "Look," I said, throwing up my hands, "you're right. I didn't want to pass Tovitch, but not because of you. He's been hassling me since Friday. Obviously the guy's not my best friend. I was afraid he'd try to ram me."

This was lame and Alex didn't buy it. "He's on your case because you hang out with me. He's calling us both fags."

I opened my mouth, then closed it, not knowing what to say. Alex slumped down with his back against the railing, gripping his knees. "No matter where I go, there's trouble," he whispered.

Rita knelt behind him, putting her hands on his shoulders. "Alex, it's not you! How many times do I have to tell you—"

He swiveled his head around to stare at her, giving her an intense look full of invisible words. Rita drew in her breath, then said, "Okay—I get the message." She stumbled down the steps, wiping her eyes, and took off toward the river.

I watched her jog down our hill, her loose hair rippling gently across her back.

"I have to tell you something," Alex said at last.

"Go right ahead." I licked my lips. It felt like the tense part of a movie, when the music shifts, and you know something scary's coming but you're not sure what it is.

Alex twisted that ring he wore, turning it around and around as if it were some kind of magic charm, and then pulled it off, cupping it in his hand. "This ring is part of the story," he said. "Want to see it?"

"Okay," I said. I held the ring carefully. It was actually two bands of silver, intertwined like loops of rope. I kept it for a second, to be polite, then gave it back fast. No way was I wearing the guy's ring.

"My friend Tito gave it to me before we left L.A.," Alex said. "He's got one just like it." Alex slid the silver bands onto his thin finger. His chin was fixed in that determined way he got on the soccer field. "I miss Tito," he said, turning away. "We've been friends since we were little. Even when we didn't go to the same schools, we always found a way to get together. We were both into sports—swimming, surfing, soccer—we'd hang out for hours and never run out of things to do or say." He paused. "You have a friend like that?"

"Yeah. Sandy—but he's away."

Alex let his hands drop between his knees and stared across the pasture. "Last spring Tito and I got into using Rollerblades. We worked up this routine—sometimes it was like dancing, sometimes we were challenging each other to do crazier and crazier stunts. We did everything at top speed, skating in narrow spaces or in and out of obstacle courses—we'd set up old milk crates, pile up trash cans to jump over, always moving in time with the music."

"Sounds exciting," I said, wishing he'd get to the point.

He smiled. "Yeah—it was. We were so hooked on it, we'd get up early on weekends to beat the crowds. We'd set up our boom box and tapes before the serious cyclists showed up, the ones who zoom past like they're going all the way to Tijuana . . ."

Alex's eyes were far away. "Our parents always complained that the boardwalk was seedy, but really, the people there were harmless: an old guy who slept in a refrigerator box; druggies whose brains got fried in the Sixties; women who wore their Halloween costumes until Christmas Day. The best skaters were these two black guys who ought to be in the Olympics; we learned most of our routines from them."

He picked up a stick and crouched on the ground, using the point like a pen. "See, the last line of buildings are next to this wide, paved area. . . ." He drew some jumbled box shapes in the dirt. "That's where we'd skate, before the people came. . . . There's a strip of sand, then the bike path . . ." He made squiggly lines with the stick. "And the beach; miles of white sand that's clean only in the early morning, after the tractors sweep the beach. Then the Pacific . . . and to the north, the Santa Monica Mountains. . . ."

He sketched some upside down Vs next to the waves. I listened, surprised. Beekman had never said much; now he'd opened up like a faucet.

"Sometimes, when Tito and I were skating in and out and around each other, slow and easy, listening to music, not working too hard, I'd look up the beach and think: It's paradise! As long as you forget the freeways and the people with no place to sleep."

He kept sketching, drawing wide circles in the dirt. "Everything was great until April," Alex went on. "One Sunday Tito and I actually attracted a crowd. We were pumped up, giving each other new ideas every few seconds, trying moves we'd never done before, spinning each other around, skating closer and closer without knocking each other down."

I plucked at a splinter in the wooden post. I was thinking about the way Alex and Rita had danced at Kai's. Did he and Tito look like that, when they skated together? Alex kept right on talking.

"We didn't realize this guy from school was there, watching us. Felix was a ratty-eyed kid; sort of like Tovitch, only smaller, meaner. The next day in school, he spread the word that Tito and I were—a couple—that we came on to each other while we were skating." Alex took a deep breath; his voice shook. "He said that when we sat on the beach afterward we got—well—physical."

I swallowed, trying to wet my throat. Alex's voice rose; the muscles in his upper arms were clenched, like tightened ropes. "Felix spoiled it! We were only putting sunscreen on each other— big deal! And lots of guys skate together—what's wrong with that?"

He was almost crying. I couldn't answer. Alex bent his head and yanked out hunks of grass by the roots, scattering them over his legs. "After that, it was like we had the word 'fag' stitched onto our shirts. If we even looked at each other in school, guys made comments. We were branded."

He stood up and came close. His eyes were red rimmed; his breath smelled sour. "Now it's happening again. And you know what the worst part is?"

I edged away, shaking my head.

"Tito's not here. There's no one to talk to. Rita tries to understand—but she can't." Beads of sweat broke out on his chin. He wiped them with his shirt and jumped off the steps, walking in circles and gulping for breath. When he glanced at me, I dropped my eyes. "It's almost like Felix called Tovitch to tip him off, before I moved to town. Do you think I'm being paranoid?"

"A little," I said, trying to lighten things up. "Tovitch was born mean. You have to ignore him."

Alex actually laughed at me. "Like you did today?"

I blushed. "Yeah. I give good advice, huh?"

"I can't figure you out," Alex said. "When I saw you fighting with Randy, I thought maybe you were sticking up for me. But then, when you tried to hide—I wasn't sure. Where do you fit in with this, anyway?"

I felt hot from my gut all the way to my neck. "I just want to play soccer," I said.

"So do I," Alex whispered. His mouth quivered; I turned away and looked down the hill. Rita was walking back toward us, with Molly behind her. They must have bumped into each other on the road.

"Here come the girls," I said.

"Fine." Alex flicked his hair off his face; his voice was steady and cool again. "When we moved, I promised

Tito I'd score a goal for him every game—one hat trick per season if I could manage it. But that's a joke, if you guys won't let me play."

"What do you mean?" I asked. "You're a starting player —you'll be on the field every minute."

His smile was thin. "I can't play alone, Todd. People have to work with me; pass me the ball."

"They do."

"Sometimes," he answered lightly. "Just watch, next practice. Tovitch tries hard to keep the ball away from me. And you help him."

"When?" I felt trapped and edgy, like I'd strapped myself into a car at the roller coaster and then decided, too late, that I wanted out. The girls were almost in earshot. "That's crazy—you're the best player we've got." When he didn't answer, I asked, "What do you want me to do?"

"Just let me play the game. Because I'm good at it— and it's all I've got left."

He turned his back and walked slowly across the drive-way to meet the girls. My stomach was in knots. Now I knew what his mother meant about Alex having trouble in L.A. The way Alex described his friend Tito reminded me of a guy talking about his girlfriend, not his best buddy. And he was wearing Tito's ring.

Did that mean Tovitch was right about Alex?

# Chapter Eleven

I went upstairs to use the bathroom. When I came down, Alex was sitting on the porch with Molly and Rita, chatting quietly.

Molly did a double take at my face. "What happened to *you*?"

I sighed. I was tired of explaining a fight that seemed more and more stupid. "I had a little run-in with Tovitch."

"You fought Randy *Tovitch*?" Molly actually looked sympathetic. "Because of Friday?" she asked.

"Not exactly." My cheeks were burning. "It's too complicated to explain."

"Want some ice?" she asked.

"No thanks—it doesn't hurt much." I cleared my throat. "I'll take you guys home now."

"Fine," Alex said, but Rita looked disappointed, and Molly complained, "Todd, not yet—Rita wants to see the pictures of my California trip."

"Whatever." I scrubbed my hair with both hands. Talk

about stuck—to get rid of Alex, I'd have to be rude to Rita. So I beckoned to Beekman. "Want a sandwich?"

"Come on," Molly said to Rita, following us into the kitchen. "My photo album's in my room."

"Don't forget to show her your pictures of Romeo," I teased.

Molly shot me a nasty look and closed the door at the foot of the stairway.

I rummaged in the fridge. "Nothing to eat in here, as usual," I muttered, pulling out a jar of peanut butter and some tiny carrots from the garden. I set them on the table, still avoiding Alex's face. I didn't know what to say to him.

"Who's Romeo?" Alex asked, opening the jar. "Does Molly have a boyfriend?"

"Yeah. Surprising, isn't it?"

"Not really. Your sister's nice."

I shrugged. What did *he* know about Molly? I yanked stuff out of the bread box until I found two bagels that actually seemed fresh. "She's hooked up with some guy named Ramon," I told Alex. "Dug him up in California this summer."

Alex dipped a carrot into the jar. "Sounds like you don't approve."

"I just like to give her a hard time. Who knows what he sees in her."

Alex looked puzzled. "Why? What's wrong with Molly?"

I cut the bagels in half and slathered them with peanut butter. "Nothing, I guess. It's just that she's my sister, so she gets on my nerves sometimes. Know what I mean?"

Alex shook his head. Of course, I realized; he wouldn't know. Alex and Rita acted different than most brothers and sisters, maybe because they were twins. Anyway, I shouldn't insult Molly, not when she'd covered for me after the accident. "She's not so bad," I admitted, glancing at the ceiling. Molly and Rita's giggles were barely muffled by the old floorboards.

"I like your sister," Alex said, pushing his hair back and giving me a clear, steady look. "She doesn't care what other people think."

He didn't say it, but I got the message loud and clear: he was spelling out the difference between Molly and me. Some nerve. I ducked into the pantry and stood there a minute until I'd cooled down, then came back with a bag of chips. I popped it between my hands, busting the chips inside, but I didn't care. Alex had a talent for making me feel uncomfortable.

"So, is this thing with Molly and Ramon pretty serious?" Alex asked.

"Why, you want to take her out?"

"No—I'm just curious," Alex said, flustered.

He opened his mouth to say something else, but I held up my hand, warning him that the girls were on their way. They came clattering downstairs. Molly's hair was pulled back so you could see her face. She'd changed into a clean shirt and was wearing some dangling earrings I'd never seen before. For a second I wondered if she'd fixed herself up for Alex's benefit. Rita, on the other hand, was one of those girls who looked pretty even in her stained soccer shirt. She smiled and spun Molly around. "Like her French braid?"

I crossed my eyes at Molly. "She doesn't look French to me."

"She looks beautiful." Blair's voice came from behind us. We turned around; Blair stood in the door of the family room. "Hello," she said. Her words came out sleepy and slow. All it took was a few hours in the darkroom to make her sound dopey.

"Blair, hi. These are the Beekman twins," Molly said, pulling her over. "Alex and Rita, this is Blair."

"Nice to meet you." Blair shook their hands, but her smile turned into a frown when she saw me. "What happened?" she asked, hurrying over and cupping her small hand under my chin.

I drew back. "A little fight," I said. "Nothing serious."

Blair's green eyes flickered, and I was grateful we had company; she wouldn't quiz me until they left. Blair chatted with the twins a second, then took the girls to the garden to pick tomatoes.

The kitchen turned sultry and quiet; the old curtains hung flat at the windows. I leaned back in my chair, feeling so groggy I barely noticed the whine of an engine coming up our hill.

"You've got visitors," Alex said quietly.

I jumped to my feet as Tovitch's blue truck squealed to a halt in our yard. "What the—" I stood there, frozen, then shoved Alex backward across the kitchen, nearly knocking him over. "Don't let him see you," I warned. I opened the door to the back stairway and pushed him up the first steps. "Stay here. I'll deal with him."

Alex's face was white with anger, but he huddled out of sight on the tiny landing. I hurried outside, letting the screen door slam behind me. I couldn't believe my eyes: Kai was climbing out of the truck, followed by Dex, who jumped from the cab and went to the back to help Kai lift her bike down. She thanked him with a big smile, then wheeled her bike over to the maple tree without even looking at me.

"Well, well. We meet again." Randy's mouth was swollen and lumpy, as if he had a wad of tobacco under his upper lip. He turned and leaned toward me, resting his arms on the open window. "Had to rescue Kai on that long hill; you know what a drag it is to pedal all the way up here." When he grinned, his lip got even more distorted. "She won't be doing that again for a while. Told me she had to say good-bye to your *sister*—but not you. Too bad she's going back to Boston tonight." He paused for a split second to let the news sink in. The truck's engine popped, and Tovitch hit the accelerator until it screamed. "Any idea why *that* happened, Mr. Speed Demon?"

Kai was leaving early? I glanced at her, but she wasn't giving anything away. She came over to me, her face smooth as glass. "Is Molly around?" she asked in her coolest, most polite voice.

"Yeah—she's in the garden. With Rita—" I added, then bit my lip as a sly smile warmed Randy's face.

When Kai disappeared around the corner of the house, Tovitch said, "So Rita's here, eh?"

I didn't answer. Dex climbed into the cab, but Tovitch stayed where he was, leaning further out the window with that smirk all over his face. "Nose a little sore?" He sounded almost friendly.

I shrugged. "Least I haven't got a fat lip."

Tovitch raised one dark eyebrow. "So, if Rita's here—"

"She's hanging out with my sister, not me," I said quickly. I raised my hand and turned to go, but Tovitch wasn't done."

"Guess that means Alex is here too."

I put my hands on the roof of his cab. "Beekman?" I said softly. "No way."

Tovitch grinned. "Beginning to see the light, eh? That's good. See you at practice." He slammed the truck into reverse and wheeled out of the yard, spattering stones into the pasture. The sheep bolted, bleating as they thundered to the bottom of the hill. I unclenched my fists. I hadn't realized how wound up I was. Alex coughed behind me; he was peering through the screen, his face pinched.

"Do I have permission to come out now?" he asked.

I went to the door, trying to smile. "Hey, take it easy. I didn't want any more fights."

"Think I can't take care of myself?" His voice was clear and pale. He went slowly down the porch steps and picked up his backpack. "I heard what you said, Todd. I thought you were different; that's why I told you about what happened in L.A. Now I'm sorry I did." He turned his back on me, then gave me one last look. "At least have the decency to keep my secrets to yourself." He straightened his shoulders and took off down the driveway.

If I'd been a nice guy, I'd have stopped him, said good-bye, told him he was wrong—at least offered him a ride home. But I just watched him walk away, his arms swinging slowly, his blond hair bouncing a little as he disappeared down the hill and over the bridge.

In a few minutes I heard the girls in the kitchen with Blair; Kai came out on the porch alone. We looked at each other for a second; then our eyes drifted apart.

"So, are we speaking again?" I asked at last.

Kai took her time coming down the steps. "Only for a minute. My parents are sending me back to Boston early, thanks to Friday night." Her eyes filled with tears.

I touched a finger to her lips, took her hand, and motioned for her to follow me to the big maple. We sat down with our backs against the tree, facing away from the house. Kai cried quietly while I held her hand and waited for her to stop.

"I'm sorry," I said. "Really. I was a total jerk. Tovitch is getting worse and worse—we had a fight today. That's why I'm so ugly now." I touched my fat nose, but Kai wasn't giving me any sympathy.

"Mom's mad at your parents, too, for not calling her back—she's gone nuts. She won't talk to them until they call to apologize."

"They didn't get the message."

Kai stared at me. "What do you mean?"

"I erased the tape after your mom called. Now Dad's away again and Blair's been working like crazy—but they'll find out soon enough. My hours are numbered."

Kai wiped her eyes. "My mother wants you out of my life. She wouldn't even let me come over here until I promised I'd only speak to Molly—"

"Gee, thanks for the loyalty."

"How else could I see you?" Kai exploded. Her eyes flashed the way they had on Friday night.

I put up my hands. "Take it easy. Listen, maybe I should call your parents and apologize to them—"

"No thanks. My mom's out of control. She'll get over it soon enough."

"I see." I was afraid to ask the next question. "Let's forget your mom for a minute—do *you* want to see me again?"

"I'm here now." She ran her fingers through the long grass. "I don't know, Todd. You're acting so strange."

"You're not exactly behaving like my girlfriend."

Kai bristled. "At least I didn't try to kill you."

I let go of her hand. "I wasn't *trying* to hurt anyone. And I said I was sorry. What more do you want?"

"That's not the only thing that made me mad," Kai said. "I was petrified when we almost crashed, but I hated the way you shoved me into that car like you were my boss." She crossed her arms. "I'm my own boss."

I laughed. "Yeah, I noticed." I glanced at the house to make sure no one was watching, then put my arm around her, drawing her head close. Her short hair prickled, clean and shiny, under my nose. "Listen, boss, don't go home mad."

"All right." Kai nestled closer and the bad vibes trickled out of her. "But what about us?" she murmured. "Will we date other people?"

I pulled away. "Do you have someone in mind?"

"Maybe." Her long eyelashes fluttered as she looked up at me. "Just teasing. But you do, don't you?"

I stretched out my legs, trying to keep my knee from bouncing. "What's that supposed to mean?"

Kai tipped her face up in that way that made her seem like she was posing for a camera. "Todd, you're so obvious—Rita walks into a room and you get bug-eyed."

Was I really that bad? I glanced toward the house, then said under my breath, "She's good-looking, but that doesn't mean I want to take her out. I'm going out with you—at least, I thought I was." When she didn't say anything, I nudged her. "Well?"

She sighed. "I'm not sure."

We were both quiet for a few minutes, thinking about what that meant. Finally she said, "Listen, we won't see each other for a few months. It's not like we're engaged or something. If we feel like dating other people, I think we should do it and not feel guilty. That's all."

"Okay," I said, but I didn't *feel* okay, just confused. Suddenly I remembered something. I pulled back so I could see right into her face. "Did Tovitch say something to you?"

She blinked. "About what?"

"Alex."

"What about him?"

Warm relief slid down into my belly. "Nothing," I said, smiling. So Tovitch had been bluffing. Jerk. Kai stood up, and I followed her.

"Molly and I are going for one last swim," she said. "But please don't come. My mom said if she heard we were together, even for fifteen minutes, she'd ground me when I get to Boston. I can't handle that."

"She's got a lot of faith in me, huh?"

Kai shook her head. "She lost it, that's all. You know how she is."

She started for the house, but I caught her sleeve. "Give me one last kiss, okay? Your mom will never know."

The lights came on in her face just for a second. "I guess."

She tasted sweet, like the grass and sunshine all around us. When I finally let her go, there was nothing more to say. That was our private good-bye for the summer.

In a few minutes Kai left to find Molly. I stayed under the tree, shading my eyes, staring into the shade. My nose was throbbing. I felt like crying but held the tears back.

"Hey, Todd," Rita called from the porch. "Where's Alex?"

"He walked home." I got up and leaned against the rough bark, keeping my distance.

Rita stared down the driveway as if she could see his shadow in the dusty ruts. "Was he okay?"

"I think so." I couldn't look at her. Maybe that twin e.s.p. stuff worked even when she and Alex were miles apart.

"That's funny," Rita said. "He doesn't usually take off without telling me."

Blair saved me then, hurrying around the side of the house with Kai and Molly, a bundle of beach towels under her arm. "Coming with us?" Blair asked as she opened the car door.

Kai caught my eyes and shook her head slightly in
warning. "Guess not," I said. I helped Kai load her bike
onto the Subaru's rack, gave her another quick hug when
I thought no one was looking, and watched her walk
around the car, her bum twitching in that way I'd always
liked. She opened her window and blew me a kiss.

"Good luck with soccer," she said as the car pulled
away.

"Thanks. I'll need that." More than you could ever
guess, I told myself. The Subaru coughed and splut-
tered, kicking up dust, leaving me alone in the hot
driveway.

The afternoon dragged. I slept a little, tried to read
one of the novels I was supposed to finish before school
started, then tossed the book across the room. "Stupid,
stupid," I said. Finally I was so restless, I decided to
make dinner. I heated water for pasta and chopped some
vegetables for sauce, but even the smell of onions frying
couldn't fix my bad mood.

At dinner I was still edgy, and when Blair asked about
my face again, I gave her so few answers that she finally
threw up her hands. "You're impossible!" she said. "It's
worse than trying to drag information out of your father."

"That's an insult," I said, which didn't help things;
Blair jumped up from the table and started slamming
cupboard doors. Time to get out of there. I took my tape
deck to the porch, holding an ice pack to my forehead. A
nasty egg had sprouted above my temple, even though I
didn't remember Tovitch clipping me in that spot. I kept
the sound low and stretched out on the swing, dangling
my legs over the arm rest. Dishes clinked inside. I was

listening to a Jethro Tull tape. The notes on the flute rose and fell, competing with the crickets in the grass. It was a peaceful evening except for the craziness inside my head.

Molly came out carrying a box of matches. She lit the citronella candle, squinting at me. "How's it feel?" she asked, pointing to my forehead.

"Sore." I turned onto my side so I could see her.

"Did you and Kai break up?" she asked.

Good old Molly; straight to the point. "Yes and no," I said. Molly's mouth twitched, like she was trying not to smile. I shifted the pack. "You never liked having us go out, did you?"

She pushed back, rocking the chair. "Not at first," she admitted. "It made me jealous because I never saw Kai. But I was getting used to it."

"Well, now you can get used to something different," I said.

"I'm sorry, Todd. Really, I am." The candle sputtered, and Molly pushed on the soft edges, smoothing its shape. The yellow light made her face look waxy and pale. "Why did you and Randy fight, anyway?"

I leaned back against the cushions. They smelled musty, the way they always did at the end of the summer. "Tovitch is bugging me," I said.

"How?" Molly asked.

I sighed. "It's not important."

She sat forward. "Come on, I won't tell anyone."

I licked my lip. Molly never gave secrets away, but I was too uptight to talk about it, even with her. "Sorry, Mol. No offense, but I don't think you'd understand."

"Thanks a lot."

I shrugged and stood up, avoiding her eyes. "I'm going to pack it in. See you in the morning." Before she could say anything else, I picked up my tape recorder and went to my room, barricading the door with a chair. I seemed to have a talent for making people angry today.

I leaned my elbows on the windowsill, jacking up the sound to full volume. Ian Anderson's flute was as crazy as the feelings zinging around inside my skull. There was only one way to survive the next few days—to play soccer as if my life depended on it.

# Chapter Twelve

I woke up the next morning feeling as if a pair of cleats had walked all over my face. I checked the mirror: *not* a pretty sight.

Blair gasped when I came downstairs. "Todd! You look terrible. Shouldn't you stay home?"

I dropped into a chair and shook my head. "We've got a scrimmage and a game this week. I can't miss practice."

She lifted my hair, checking the lump on my forehead. "Hey," I complained, pulling away. "That hurts."

"Sorry." She made coffee and poured my favorite mixture—a little coffee and a lot of hot milk—into a traveling cup, spooning in extra sugar. "You'd better dose yourself with this—and take some aspirin." She sat down across from me, moving the stack of newspapers on the table. "Is there something you'd like to talk to me about? Or you could call Mark. He has a phone on the job now."

I couldn't think of anything worse than trying to explain the mess I was in to Dad while carpenters hammered in the background. "No thanks," I said, pouring cereal and milk into a bowl. "I'm okay." I tried to eat but gave up fast. It was much too early to look at food.

"You don't seem okay to me." When I didn't answer, Blair snapped a lid on the cup and handed it to me as I carried my gym bag outside. "Drive carefully," she said. "And please come home right after practice—I need the car."

"Fine."

She smiled. "You've been awfully agreeable about sharing the Subaru lately. I appreciate it."

"No problem." I tucked in my chin and headed for the door. If Blair was going out with the car, that could mean the end of my lucky streak. I couldn't expect her to stay locked in the darkroom forever. Sooner or later she'd hear the news—and then I was doomed.

Everyone at practice was stiff, nervous, and edgy, but I decided I was just going to play soccer and show Crawford I was first-string material. When we ran laps, chipping our balls in front of us, I almost kept up with Alex, even though his fast, easy pace made my lungs burn. I focused my concentration when we took shots on goal, getting it past the keeper once and coming close a second time. Of course, it was hard to ignore Tovitch. He wedged himself in line behind Alex and whispered taunts in his ear just before Beekman's turn to shoot. Alex got flustered, stumbled when he dribbled, and shot the ball so wide, the goalie didn't even need to lunge for it.

When we took a water break, I said hello to Beekman,

but all I got back was a polite nod. Forget it, I told myself. Just play the game.

After an hour of drills I was actually feeling pumped up and psyched for the scrimmage, but Crawford was grim. "Come on, *hustle!*" he yelled, jogging close behind us as we dribbled the ball around the field, once, twice, three times. "There's a *game* this week."

As if we could forget. Every step I took, I felt knife twists in my side. When Crawford gave me five minutes for a drink, I staggered to the bench next to Craig and held my head over my knees, gasping for breath. "This is painful," I said.

Craig gave me a cold look, stood up slowly, and left the bench to stand by the bleachers. My stomach clenched up tight. So I was still on *his* blacklist too.

After the break the coach sent us down the field in lines of three, bringing the defense up to meet us as we charged the goal. The coach picked Tovitch, Alex, and Dex for the first line. I watched carefully. Alex was right; Tovitch and Dexter passed only to each other. Twice Tovitch kicked it straight to a defender, and the offense lost control—even though Alex had managed to maneuver himself into an isolated position on the wing, calling, "Pass, Randy! Over here!"

Ozzie bounced with frustration in the goal box. "Beekman was clear!" he yelled.

For once Crawford came down hard on Tovitch. "Randy," he called from the sidelines, "pass it off." Tovitch raised his hand in a salute.

"Give me a break," Drew muttered, coming over to

talk to me. "What's Tovitch trying to do? He'd better not pull that trick in a game. Crawford still lets him off too easy."

Crawford glanced our way; had he heard us? He whirled back to watch the field from under the brim of his cap, punching the air with his right fist as he barked directions. "Alex, stay at left wing," he called. "Drew take the right." He waved at us. "Todd, go in at striker."

Drew glanced at me. "Uh, oh," he said softly.

We hustled out. I would have called it a perfect front line—Drew, Alex, and me—except I could feel Randy's scowl bore into my back as I ran down the field. I forgot about him in seconds, though, because playing with Alex was a dream. Even if I kicked the ball too far ahead, or misjudged my shot somehow, Beekman managed to be there. He'd dribble so close to the defender you were sure they'd collide, then dodge him at the last minute, like a guy playing professionally. He made it seem so easy—his arms were loose and limp, his hair tossed lightly, his legs so long they seemed to amble or dance— and he never lost control of the ball.

"Man on!" Drew warned as the sweeper charged. Alex did a little slide to the right, keeping the ball with him, and kicked it all the way to the far side of the field. Drew and the fullback fought over the ball. Drew kept control and took a shot on goal that missed, but only by a hair.

"Nice play!" Crawford called from the sidelines. "Let me see more of that." He beamed at Alex as we left the field, making room for the next line of three. "Great pass, Alex," he said, "nice control. Way to go, Drew; a few inches to the right and you'd have a score." He nodded at me. "A little more accuracy in your passes. I still think your best spot is midfield."

I frowned, and Crawford surprised me by putting a hand on my shoulder, speaking so the guys couldn't hear. "That's not an insult," he said. "I told you before: we need someone with your stamina at center mid. It's a tough position, but you can handle it."

"Thanks," I said, determined to go home and practice my passing anyway.

When I went for a drink, Drew asked, "Is that a possible front line—you, me, and Alex?" he asked.

"Doesn't sound like it. Crawford just said I might play center midfield."

"That's cool too. You can send them up to us." Drew tipped the thermos, filling his cup. I paced up and down near the bench. If Alex hadn't come to town, I realized, the front line would be Tovitch, Drew, and me. I gouged a divot of grass from the sidelines with my heel and took some deep breaths, trying to relax, but it didn't work. I was too pumped up.

Tovitch was out there again; he took a shot on goal and missed. Drew stood beside me, wiping his mouth. "Tovitch still won't let Alex near the ball," Drew said. "Who's going to wake him up?"

Before I could answer, Crawford called, "O'Connor, back on the field."

I jogged into position. This time Crawford's lineup made me real jittery: Tovitch on *right* wing, Alex at striker, me on the left. Tovitch didn't like it; he wouldn't hold his position. "Randy!" Alex yelled, passing over to him, then running ahead. Alex kept himself clear for a return kick, but Tovitch hogged the ball all the way down the field, took a shot on goal from too far out, and swore when the ball sailed easily into the keeper's waiting arms.

"Tovitch, if you can't pass, get off the field!" Crawford roared.

"Hey." Tovitch looked shocked. He jogged over to the coach, his face ruddy and streaked with sweat. "I'm not used to *right* wing."

"Tough," Crawford said. "It's good practice; you need to use your right foot more. You too, O'Connor," he said to me. "Now get back out there, same line. Try again."

On our second run, I booted the ball to Alex, who spurted down the field. Craig ran to head him off, but Alex dodged, drew back, faked a move toward Tovitch and then fooled the defense by sending the ball across his body, back to me. I scrambled for it, surprised; kept it a few seconds as we neared the goal, then looked for an opening. The defense was closing in. "Back to the keeper!" Ozzie cried to the fullbacks, dancing in and out of the goal box. Alex moved into a space; as the ball left my foot, Tovitch appeared out of nowhere. The ball disappeared in a scramble of bodies and I heard an ugly sound as someone's foot connected with flesh. Alex went down, the ball shot out of the muddle toward the goal, and Ozzie lunged, missing it by a few inches.

Tovitch danced away from the tangle, raising his fist to claim credit for the goal. The rest of us froze, then edged toward Alex, who writhed on the ground. Craig knelt

beside Beekman, helping him sit up. Crawford ran over
and crouched next to Alex. "What happened?"

Alex drew up his right leg, his face twisted as he
kneaded his thigh. "I got clipped—bad charley horse.
Better in a minute," he said, gritting his teeth.

Crawford bent down, inspecting the leg. Cleat marks
branded the skin. "Drew, get the ice pack." The coach's
blue eyes searched the circle until they found Tovitch.
"That was dangerous kicking, Randy," the coach said.
"You don't need a ref to tell you that."

Randy's eyes widened. "*I* did that? Sorry, Beekman.
It was an accident." Alex didn't look up. The rest of us
shifted uneasily and some guys drifted toward the bench
for water.

"It was intentional." Craig's voice was quiet but fierce
as he faced Tovitch down. "You did it on purpose. I saw
you. That kick was aimed."

Crawford stepped between them. "Easy." His eyes
flickered over Randy's face. "Is that true?"

Tovitch dropped the ball, shaking his head. "No way.
Why would I kick Beekman? He's our *star*, isn't he?"

The words stuck to his tongue like something sickly
sweet. Crawford rubbed his chin, pacing in a circle
around Alex, who was still working the muscle with his
fingers. When Drew draped the ice pack over Alex's leg,
Beekman gave him a half smile and stood up slowly,
holding the pack to his thigh. Crawford put out a hand to
steady him, but Alex brushed him off.

"I'm all right, Coach," he said quietly. "I'll just put the
leg up a minute." He limped toward the bench with
Craig beside him.

"Tovitch, you stay here," the coach said. His voice was tight and sharp. "The rest of you, beat it. Take a few more shots on goal."

"Hey," Tovitch protested. "It was an accident—"

Crawford frowned, shutting him up. We couldn't hear what Crawford was saying, but it must have been bad. When we turned around at the far end of the field, the coach was pacing, slicing the air with the side of one hand while Tovitch stood with his head down.

"Think the coach will bench him for the first game?" Drew asked, jogging beside me.

"Hope not," I said.

Drew seemed puzzled. "Lucky that kick didn't catch Alex any higher," he said. "Knowing Tovitch, that's probably where he was aiming."

I winced. "Maybe. With so many guys on the ball, I couldn't see what was happening. It's hard to believe Tovitch would actually try to hurt Alex."

Drew snorted. "Right, O'Connor. Whose side are you on, anyway?"

"Whose *side*?" I asked carefully. "I didn't know there were sides. I'm just trying to play the game."

Drew shook his head as if he didn't believe me and took a position at the other end of the line as we set ourselves up for shots on goal.

In a few minutes Tovitch joined us. His face was flushed but plastered with a look that said: Who cares?

"He give you hell?" Dexter asked as Tovitch barged his way into line.

"Naw," Tovitch said. "Just benched me for tomorrow.

Too bad for the team—hate to see you lose, even if it is only a scrimmage. Here, let me have a go at the ball, will you?"

"What a swelled head," Drew muttered. Tovitch wasn't listening; he'd already cut into line ahead of Dex. He steamed toward the goal with his body leaning forward, and aimed a perfect, right-footed kick into the far corner of the net. Ozzie's fingers ticked the leather, but the ball sailed past him. Tovitch ran back grinning.

"See what I mean?" he laughed. "I can even do it right-footed. You guys don't have a chance without me."

"We don't have a chance without Beekman, either," Drew said quietly.

Tovitch hooted. "Why Drew—another faggot in our midst?"

Drew's freckled face turned a deep red-brown as Rich and Dexter and a few other defenders joined in the laughter. I glanced at the bench, wondering if Alex could hear us. He was on his feet now, stretching, while Craig and the coach hovered over him.

"Is Beekman really hurting?" Rich asked.

Tovitch chuckled. "Not as much as he would be if I'd caught him any higher."

"Nasty," Rich said, but he laughed too.

Drew shot me a look. *What did I tell you?* I could hear him ask silently.

I was next in line; Tovitch punched my arm as he jogged by, and whispered in my ear, "See? I did you a favor. With any luck, we'll still end up on the front line together."

"Maybe." I felt pulled in a thousand different directions. Luckily Crawford blew the whistle and motioned us back to the bench.

When we were clustered around him, the coach checked his watch and said, "I've got teachers' meetings today, so I'll only keep you a minute." He started pacing, his stocky legs punching the ground with each step. "I'm not happy with what I see out there. Ball hogging, sloppy passes, not enough teamwork. We've got a scrimmage tomorrow, with Central Valley High, only one practice after that. The scrimmage doesn't count in the standings, but it counts with me." He glanced around the circle, his blue eyes sharp. "Where's the keeper?"

"Here, sir." Ozzie's gloved hand waved from the back. He was taller than everyone else except Beekman.

"Come up here." Ozzie pushed forward, looking worried, and Crawford smiled for once. "Hey, take it easy," he said. "I'm making you captain."

Ozzie's long face relaxed and he took a deep breath. "Thanks, Coach."

I glanced at Tovitch. As top senior player, he might have expected to be at least co-captain. His face looked dark and heavy; he watched the far side of the field.

"Some of you guys have forgotten you're a team," Crawford said. "Ozzie still remembers."

I shifted uneasily from one foot to the other. That slice was aimed at all of us, and it cut me right in the gut.

"Take your uniforms home," Crawford went on. "I want them clean and white tomorrow. Alex, get some heat on that charley horse—massage it if you can. We don't want you on the injured list."

He studied his clipboard, then said to Ozzie, "You'll have one less starting player at the scrimmage. Tovitch will be on the bench. I don't allow dangerous play on the field, even when there are no refs here to call it." Crawford's cool gaze skimmed over us before he zipped up his windbreaker and stalked away toward the school.

# Chapter Thirteen

No one said much as we gathered up our gear. I expected Tovitch to head for his truck, but he went straight to the locker room, whistling a low tune under his breath. Craig caught my eye. "Going home?" he asked in a neutral voice.

"In a minute. I've got to get my uniform." I hustled after the rest of the guys. If Craig was trying to find a ride for Alex, I couldn't deal with that now.

When I opened the door, Randy's raspy voice echoed off the tiles in the open shower. He was scrubbing his hair under the water jet, making comments to Dexter and Rich as they toweled off. Drew stood alone in the far shower. I twisted the dial on my combination lock, eager to get out of there before Tovitch was done, but I wasn't fast enough. He came out dripping as I rummaged around for my uniform. Tovitch swaggered across the room with nothing on, grabbed a towel and wrapped it around his waist, then stood on tiptoe near the tiny window and pushed it open.

"What do you know?" he announced. "Cool dude Beekman has to wait *outside* the locker room." He turned so we could see his face. His black eyebrows looked greased from the shower. "Ooo," he cried, flicking his towel open to show a quick flash of butt, then cinching it tight around his waist again. "You guys notice Beekman never comes in here?"

Everyone was suddenly quiet. It was true.

"So maybe he doesn't like the locker room." Craig sidled along a bench and sat down to undo his cleats. "It stinks in here. Anyway, what do you care?"

Tovitch grinned, obviously enjoying his audience. "Maybe it's too exciting for Alex, to be in the same room with so many hunks. Huh, guys?"

This time even Rich and Dex looked uncomfortable. They started rummaging in their lockers for clothes, covering themselves up. Tovitch smirked at me. "What do you think, O'Connor? Notice the way he's snagged both our positions?"

"He plays better than we do," I said. The truth, but it sounded lame.

Tovitch rubbed himself dry. "We'll see how well he does with a sore leg," he said, and pulled on his shorts.

"Tovitch, shut up!" We turned around. Drew stood at the edge of the tiled floor, water running down his freckled chest and shoulders. With his hair plastered to his skull he looked small but fierce. The walls of the locker room pressed in on all of us. "You could wreck this team, Tovitch, ever think of that?"

Tovitch flicked his towel at Drew. "More recruits for the lady's club, eh? Maybe you're the one to give Beekman that nice massage the coach recommended. . . ."

Drew raised his fists, but Craig yelled, "Cool it, guys!" He ran along the benches and jumped between them, his hands wedged against their bare chests. "Are you nuts? We've had enough fights. Let's be a team for once."

"Yeah," Rich drawled, slamming his locker. We all turned to him, surprised. He usually went along with Tovitch, but this time his fleshy face was red and angry. "Tone it down, Tovitch," he said. "You want to miss the first *game*, too? We need you out there."

Tovitch scrubbed his hair and muttered something under his breath. Craig leaned close. "Want to say that out loud?" Craig challenged.

Tovitch shrugged. "I was just wondering"—he looked at me, then at the rest of the team—"why Todd doesn't ask Beekman what kind of troubles he had in L.A."

Something sour slid down my throat. I picked up my cleats and tucked my uniform under my arm. How fast could I get out of here?

"What are you talking about?" Drew demanded, edging between the benches until he and Craig made a sandwich on either side of Tovitch.

Randy's smile made my skin crawl. "Todd knows what I mean," he said. "Don't you, O'Connor?"

I shook my head. "Afraid not."

I was halfway out the door when Tovitch called, "Todd, you forgot something." He held up my ball with my name scrawled across it in magic marker. It wobbled when he tossed it to me; it was leaking air. "So you're still in tight with the fag," Tovitch said.

"If you're so curious, ask him yourself," I said, turning my back fast so no one could see my face.

I slammed the door behind me and hurried to my car. My gut churned. How the hell did Tovitch know about Alex and L.A.? Then I remembered: the morning Mrs. Beekman spoke to me, Tovitch had overheard her asking me to bring the twins home. That's when she'd said "Alex went through some hard times in L.A. . . ." Tovitch must have heard that, too.

I fumbled with the hatchback, wondering how many guys were watching from that stupid little window. The weird thing was, I could imagine their faces, each set of accusing eyes, but I couldn't picture my own. Every part of me was a blur. I was missing, somehow; as deflated as the soccer ball tucked under my arm.

Before I climbed into my car, I took a quick look around to make sure Alex had gone. I congratulated myself; the Beekmans' Chevy was pulling out into traffic with their mother at the wheel. I was shocked to open the door of my car and find Rita slumped in the passenger's seat, snuffling and wiping her nose.

I sucked in my breath. "Rita!" I stared at her, then tossed my gear into the backseat. "You surprised me. Is something wrong?"

She made a funny noise that was half a sob, half laughter. "What do you think? Everything's wrong!" She refused to look at me, even when I tore a piece of paper towel off a dirty roll and shoved it under her nose. "I have to talk to you," she said. "Can we get out of here, please?"

"Sure," I mumbled, and started the car. In all my fantasies about being alone with Rita, this wasn't the way I'd pictured things at all. "I have to take the car home first. Blair needs it."

"Fine," she said. "We'll go to your house."

I didn't want to hang out in the lot, not with the guys about to spill out of the locker room, so I wheeled across the pavement and turned toward home. Rita kept her eyes on her lap; she obviously had no intention of telling me what was bugging her. Of course, I had a pretty good idea what was on her mind.

There weren't any tapes that were right for my foul mood, so I just watched the road, taking each curve slow and easy. When we crossed our bridge, Rita put a hand on my arm and said, "Can you stop here? I don't want to talk to you with Molly around."

I slowed up, so nervous my knee jiggled the steering wheel. "Okay," I said. "Let me run the car up to Blair—"

"I'll wait," she said, and jumped out.

It took me a while to find Rita when I came back down the hill. She'd followed the path beside the river and was sitting under the big white pine near the pool where Sandy and I liked to fish, chewing on a long piece of grass. She wasn't one of those girls who look pretty when they cry—her nose was still swollen, and her eyes were red. But at least she wasn't sniffling anymore.

I took a few steps closer. She couldn't hear me; the river made too much noise. I stood still, watching as she raised her hands to pull the elastic from her hair. I had this sudden urge to kneel beside her and comb out the tangles with my fingers. I'd start at her neck, part the silver strands slowly and carefully, loosening each snarl all the way to her waist. I'd take off my shirt and let her hair swish across my chest, going crazy with its silky softness, or hold it to my face, forgetting everything that had happened since she moved here . . .

"Hey!" Rita whirled around suddenly. "Don't sneak up on me like that—you scared me."

"Sorry." Her eyes had gone to a deep, shadowy blue, like curtains drawn across a window; I couldn't tell what she was thinking. I tossed a stone into the river. It splashed in the shallows with a hollow thunk.

"Listen," I said, "I'm sorry about Alex—"

"You should be." Rita sat up straight and clenched her hands. "He told you about Tito, right?"

I nodded, shifting from one foot to the other. Beekman's story was trailing behind me like a bad smell.

"Alex trusted you," she whispered, her voice shaking again. "We both did." She looked up at me, her eyes accusing. "We thought you were our friend."

"I am," I protested, but she shook her head sadly. "Alex is a great guy," I went on, even though I knew it sounded phony. "Really. And he's an amazing soccer player. I like you both a lot." I blushed, and Rita stared at me until I was so uncomfortable I had to slide down the bank to get away.

When Rita stood up, the feathery pine needles brushed her head. "If you were Alex's friend, you wouldn't have made him hide on the stairs—"

"That's not fair!" I chucked a heavy stone into the

stream; it ricocheted off a boulder. "I told Alex, I was just trying to protect him! I didn't want Tovitch to beat *him* up too!"

"Bullshit," Rita said. "You're lying." I sucked in my breath, feeling a pain deeper than anything Tovitch could have inflicted on me.

"You're just trying to protect yourself." Rita's voice rose over the hum of the water. "You're so obvious, Todd; it's pathetic." She snapped a branch from the tree and stripped the needles with her long fingers. "It could be so different," she said softly.

"How?" I was almost crying with frustration myself. "It's Tovitch, can't you see? *He's* the one who's making our lives miserable!"

"You don't have to go along with his name calling."

I kicked some loose stones aside. The river lapped at my heels. I took a deep breath and met her eyes. "I've never called Alex a fag," I said.

Rita winced and her eyes filled. "So why won't you stand up for him?"

Because I'm a chicken, I thought, licking my lips. My throat felt taut, as if she'd slipped a noose around it. Rita skidded down the bank and took my hand. Her eyes were so intense, I wasn't sure if she was going to slap my face—or kiss me. I steeled myself, but she just said softly, "You could change everything. And you know what's really sad? I thought you and I could be friends. I don't mean like you and Kai; I don't want to mess that up—but we could talk, and the four of us could even hang out together—you and Molly, Alex and me. But that's impossible now. Because when you're mean to

Alex, you're mean to me. If he hurts, I feel it inside my own body. Right here." She pulled my hand to her chest, right below her breasts. Her heart skipped against my fingers, making my cheeks burn as if she'd slapped me.

"I'm not trying to hurt you," I said in a hoarse voice.

"But you are." Rita let go. "Just do me one small favor. Treat my brother like a human being. That's all I ask." She climbed the bank to the path and headed toward the road.

"Wait a second," I called, scrambling after her. "Where are you going?"

"To Randy's." She didn't look at me.

"Are you crazy? You want to get yourself killed?"

"Randy won't hurt me." She was jogging now. I ran to keep up with her. "He's afraid of girls," she said.

"Wait," I said, grabbing her shirt.

She shoved me away. "Leave me alone. I know what I'm doing—and I don't need your help. Not when you're on Randy's side."

"I'm not!"

Rita gave me one last look. Her eyes were deep with sadness. "Prove it," she said, and left me standing in the middle of our dusty driveway.

# Chapter Fourteen

I watched Rita cross the bridge, her hair switching from side to side across her back. She turned left on the town road and disappeared in the shade of the maples. Apparently she already knew the way to Randy's.

"What the hell," I whispered to myself. Rita was probably right. Tovitch wouldn't hurt her; he'd be too embarrassed. But what if he made some rude remark, or ran his hand down her back, the way he'd done with Kai? I decided to follow, keeping my distance so she wouldn't know I was behind her. I drew back when I came around the first bend, slowing my pace and sticking to the bank. She was walking at a fast clip, her head held high like she wasn't afraid of anything. What was she planning to do— tell Tovitch off?

Randy's coon hound bayed as I came around the last corner. I ducked behind a tree. Rita stood just a few yards in front of me, her fists clenched. She wouldn't know the dog was chained. Mr. Tovitch's huge log truck

was parked in the dooryard, so top-heavy it looked ready
to tip over. A big horse trailer with its tailgate open was
sitting near the barn, but there was no sign of Randy's
blue pickup. I licked my lips, remembering how nervous
I used to be when I was a kid and had to bike past here
to get to Sandy's. I always pedaled with my chin tucked
under, praying no one would see me. I didn't feel much
braver now.

I waited, wondering what Rita would do next, when
someone shouted angrily from inside the horse trailer. A
high-pitched squeal bounced around the metal box, and
something pounded against the sides like a sledgeham-
mer gone wild. A voice rose in ugly curses, and the
whole rig swayed and gyrated as if there were a brawl
going on.

Rita froze and I ran up beside her, grabbing her hand.
She let out a tiny scream but I hushed her. "Move it," I
hissed, pulling her up the bank and into the bushes.
"Mr. Tovitch is a nasty guy." I pushed on her shoulders.
"Get down, so he can't see you." Rita's eyes widened,
but she obeyed me, ducking behind a tree. She was
shaking.

"You want to get killed?" the voice roared. The squeal
turned into a desperate whinny that gave me goose-
bumps. Hooves beat against the floorboards and the
cussing got worse. The racket was deafening, even
though we were on the other side of the road.

"Holy, moly," I whispered. I turned to Rita, speaking
as quietly as I could. "How about getting out of here?"

She shook her head. "We should do something."

"Like what? No one messes with Randy's dad." Just

then a horse's big rear end appeared at the edge of the ramp and a pair of enormous hooves scrambled unsteadily on the metal lip.

"Git down, you lazy good-for-nothing bonehead!" Mr. Tovitch yanked at the horse's halter, trying to back it down the ramp. When the horse balked, he beat its neck and shoulder with a heavy stick.

"This is terrible." Rita grabbed my arm. The horse reared, almost hitting its head on the roof of the trailer, and for a second I thought it might pull the whole rig over. The more the horse tossed its head, the more Mr. Tovitch lashed out at him. Finally, the muscles on its neck rippling with fear, the huge chestnut backed slowly down the ramp, shaking the rickety panels with each heavy step. When it reached the ground, it turned toward the road; its eyes were wild, and foamy streaks spread across its withers. The horse strained and lunged as Mr. Tovitch dragged it toward the pasture gate. When the horse tried to break loose, Mr. Tovitch slapped it again, using the butt end of the lead rope this time.

Rita turned to me. "He's horrible," she said, shuddering. "We should call someone."

"Wait," I whispered. Mr. Tovitch maneuvered the chestnut into the pasture. He let the horse loose, and the two of them stood there a minute, eyeing each other. Then he turned on his heel and left the chestnut in its harness. The horse trembled all over, its thick, heavy head shifting quickly from side to side as if it were waiting for the next blow. Mr. Tovitch shut the pasture gate, pulled a beer bottle from the cab, and drained it in a few swallows, then limped into the house.

Rita burst into tears. "The horse is bleeding. How can anyone treat an animal that way?" She stood up. "You were right; this was a stupid idea. I'm getting out of here."

I started toward the road, then ducked down. "Too late," I whispered, pulling her deeper into the brush with me. "Here comes Tovitch. Stay low. We don't want him to know we've been spying on his dad."

Randy's blue truck rattled toward us, its rear end fishtailing on the washboard at the corner. He pulled in behind the trailer, jumped out, and went straight for the horse. He climbed the fence and stood in the pasture a minute, shaking his head.

The chestnut pawed the ground with its front hoof. One of the long leather traces from the harness was tangled around its leg. I parted the branches to get a better look. Tovitch walked carefully toward the horse, talking in a soft, almost crooning voice, like someone putting a baby to sleep.

The chestnut looked ready to bolt, but Tovitch just inched toward it, every step slow and easy, keeping up a gentle patter until he had hold of the halter. Even then he didn't stop talking; he stroked the horse's neck for a long time, then slowly moved his hand along his back, over the withers, up the mane, and behind the ears, his voice so calm and steady, it seemed as if the horse were hypnotized.

I glanced at Rita; she was kneeling in the dirt, her eyes big and round, her hands resting on her bare knees. My legs were killing me from crouching in a crooked position, but I didn't dare budge. We watched Tovitch tie the horse to the fence and unbuckle the heavy harness from under its belly and chest. He slid the traces off the horse's back, pulling the tail away gently, soothing him as he worked. Even from across the road, we could see dark lines on the horse where sweat had formed under the leather straps.

Tovitch picked up a bucket, filled it at an outdoor spigot, and held it to the horse's muzzle, letting him drink it down. Then he disappeared into the barn.

"Let's split," I whispered to Rita.

She shook her head. "Wait," she said.

Tovitch came out of the barn with a rag and a big sponge shaped like a doughnut. He dipped it into the bucket and sponged down the chestnut, carefully cleaning its neck, shoulders, back and legs. When he washed its belly, he hummed softly.

I turned to Rita, raising my eyebrows, and she shook her head in disbelief. Who would ever expect to see Randy Tovitch being so gentle? He had the animal so relaxed, it swished its tail and craned its neck over the fence to nibble at weeds. Except for the blood on its neck, you'd never know there'd been a struggle.

When it seemed as if we'd been there forever, Tovitch finished drying the horse and took everything back into the barn. I stood up. "Now's your chance," I said. "I'll show you the way back through the woods if you want."

But Rita was already headed down the bank. She sauntered across the road and leaned against the fence, leaving me with two awkward choices: I could crouch in the bushes and look like a fool if Tovitch spotted me, or make it seem as if I'd been out walking with Rita. Feeling like an idiot, I stumbled into the middle of the road as Tovitch came out of the barn. He carried a bundle of hay under his arm. His eyes narrowed into two black points when he saw us.

He glanced at Rita, looking slightly embarrassed, then turned to me. "Well, well," he said after a minute. "Look who's out walking. Lost your car privileges?"

I shrugged, trying to stay nonchalant. "Not yet. Blair still hasn't heard—guess she'll find out soon enough, especially if you keep blabbing about it."

Tovitch shook the hay loose under the horse's muzzle; it watched us nervously, then began to nibble the dry grass.

Rita reached out her hand, touching the tangled mane between the horse's ears. "He's beautiful," she said. "What's his name?"

Tovitch seemed startled; he probably wasn't expecting her to be friendly. "Suzy," Tovitch told her. "She's a mare. Want to pat her?" He tugged the chestnut's halter, bringing her closer. Rita hesitated, then touched the horse's soft muzzle. Her nostrils widened and she wrinkled her upper lip, revealing a band of yellow teeth. Rita snatched her hand away and Tovitch laughed. "Scared you, huh?"

"Sort of," Rita admitted. "I'm not used to horses. We didn't see too many in L.A."

Tovitch scratched the horse between her ears. She stopped eating and rubbed her nose up and down his leg.

"She likes you," Rita said.

Tovitch kept fussing with the horse; he seemed uncomfortable.

"What happened to her neck?" Rita asked innocently, pointing to the place where blood had bubbled and clotted just below the tangled mane.

"Must have got into something in the woods," Tovitch muttered. "I've got some ointment to put on her"—he pulled a tube from his pocket—"but she'll be more likely to stand quiet with no one else around. If you get the point."

"I'll take off in a minute," Rita said, but she stood still.

Tovitch glanced at her and his face reddened. Rita was right; Tovitch didn't know how to act with a girl up that close.

"It's funny," Rita said slowly, her hands trembling where she clutched the railing, "how you can be so kind to your horse—but so mean to my brother."

Tovitch opened his mouth to say something, but Rita kept right on talking. "Please stop what you're doing to Alex," she begged, and then she turned to me, her face crumpling. "Stop it, both of you. Don't you see how cruel you are?" Her voice broke. "As for you, Todd O'Connor, you're just a big hypocrite. Don't follow me again." She whirled around and ran awkwardly down the road, her elbows clenched to her sides.

I stood there a second, too stunned to know what to do next. Tovitch leaned across the railing, coming so close I could smell his rank breath. "Man, the guy must be really desperate, to pull a stunt like this one," he said.

"What do you mean?" I asked.

"Siccing his sister on me—that's pretty wimpy. You'd

think he could handle his own fights." He shifted the horse's mane and squeezed a long film of ointment onto the biggest cut. The horse shuddered and skittered sideways. "Steady," he said quietly.

"I don't think Alex knew she was coming," I said, although I had no idea if he did or not. "I sure wouldn't want my sister handling my problems."

Tovitch laughed. "Your sister might deal with things better than you do, O'Connor."

I didn't like the way this conversation was headed. "Keep Molly out of this, all right?" I said.

"Sure." Tovitch sponged the horse's neck again, carefully loosening another clot. "Listen," he said, "now that we're alone—why don't you tell me if you've asked Alex about L.A."

I opened my mouth, then closed it. I saw Rita's haunted eyes; heard her voice begging me to treat her brother as a human being. "I don't know any more than you do," I hedged, and then asked quickly, "Why'd you kick him, anyway?"

Tovitch didn't answer for a minute. He squeezed another long ribbon of ointment onto the horse's cut, keeping a tight hold on its halter with the other hand.

"Why do you think? The guy was playing striker." Tovitch capped the ointment, then reached for the sponge and ran it down the mare's front legs. "If we give Beekman enough grief, maybe he'll quit."

"You're nuts," I said.

Tovitch moved to the mare's back legs. "Still standing up for the faggot, eh?"

I looked around quickly, to make sure Rita was really

gone. "Of course not," I said. "But it sounds like you'd rather lose a game than have Alex play."

"Who says we'd lose? We had a great team before Beekman showed up, and we can have one again, even if he quits."

I bent to pick a stalk of grass and chewed it nervously. "Crawford's watching you," I said. "You'd better be careful, or you might be the one who's off the team."

Tovitch rubbed the back of his wrist over his mouth. "I know what I'm doing." His upper lip curled over his chipped tooth. "Crawford would never keep me from playing. Especially when he sees how badly you do without me in the scrimmage."

I chucked the grass aside. "God, you've got a fat head."

Tovitch shrugged. "Better than an empty one."

If he meant mine, I wasn't taking the bait. Suddenly the front door slammed and Randy's face turned white. His eyes were full of fear; something I'd never seen before. "My dad," he hissed. "Beat it, if you know what's good for you."

I didn't need to be told twice. I took off down the road, running so fast my heart was hammering when I rounded the first bend. I slowed down when I was out of sight of the house, gasping for breath. Until this minute I'd always assumed Tovitch wasn't afraid of anything. Now I knew differently. For a second I wondered if Randy's dad ever hit him the way he beat his horse. The thought made me shudder. I started jogging again and didn't stop until I reached the bridge.

Rita had disappeared. I held onto the railing and watched the river a second, waiting for my breath to

slow before I climbed the hill. It was almost Labor Day
weekend, and what did I have to show for the last few
weeks of summer? All the girls angry with me, my uncle's car screwed up, our team a mess—and no friends
left.

"A great track record, O'Connor," I told myself, dragging my feet toward the house. I was hoping, in my
last-ditch fantasy way, that Rita would be waiting for me
on the porch, but the screen door stood half open, and
the house was quiet. I made myself a sandwich, but I
wasn't even hungry. Finally I flopped on the couch and
went into the last place I felt safe—deep into that empty
space called sleep.

# Chapter Fifteen

I woke up with a nasty crick in my neck; the phone was ringing in the kitchen. I limped across the room and yanked it off the hook.

" 'Lo."

"Todd?"

I swallowed a yawn. "That's right."

"Uncle Gordo. Sounds like I woke you up."

"No problem." I scrubbed my face with my free hand, trying to remember why he might be calling.

"It's about the car," he said.

Oh, yeah. *Oh* yeah. "What did they say?" I asked.

Uncle Gordo cleared this throat. "Well, there's a little more damage than we thought. They'll have to repaint the whole door, and the exhaust system's screwed up. The estimate's up to at least six hundred, with parts and labor."

"Oh." My summer earnings were sliding away like a load of stone let loose from a dump truck.

"Don't panic," Uncle Gordo said. "I have insurance.

After you pay the deductible, they'll take care of the rest. Trouble is, my deductible's fairly steep—a hundred and fifty bucks."

When I didn't say anything, he asked, "Did you faint?"

"No, I'm here; just trying to wake up. I'll send you a check tomorrow. Will the car look okay when it's done?"

"Sure," he said. "Good as new. I'll make sure you get a private viewing."

For some reason this made me feel guilty all over again. "I'm sorry," I said for the hundredth time.

"So am I," he said, then asked, "How's everything else going?"

"Lousy," I answered without even thinking.

"Yeah? What's up?"

"Oh, nothing much—just a lot of bad luck all at once."

"Sometimes talking about it changes a bad streak to a good one." He paused. "I'm good at keeping secrets, too."

All of a sudden I was sick of having the whole thing roll around inside me like a heavy ball knocking against my ribs. "Remember that guy I told you about when you were here—Randy Tovitch?"

"Sure," Uncle Gordo said. "The one who tried to steal your girl. Did he succeed?"

"Sort of—I mean, Kai and I broke up; that's part of the mess. And Tovitch is still off the wall, throwing insults around—" I hesitated.

"What kind of insults?" Uncle Gordo asked gently.

I decided to plunge right in. "He was calling me a fag, among other things. We had a big fight Monday—"

Uncle Gordo grunted, as if he'd been socked in the gut. "Who fought?" he asked. "You and Tovitch?"

"Yeah," I said. "My face still looks like pepperoni pizza." I paced the kitchen as I talked, pulling the cord to its full length, then letting it yank me back in the other direction when I reached the end.

Uncle Gordo coughed. "Was that why you chased after him the other night?"

"That was part of it."

Uncle Gordo didn't say anything for a minute, but I could hear his breath coming fast and harsh into the phone, like he was standing next to me. "This Tovitch kid—why is he picking on you?"

"It's not me so much as Alex, and anyone who hangs out with him," I said. "The first few days, when I gave Alex rides, Tovitch said that made *me* a fag too—"

"Who's Alex?" Uncle Gordo's voice was getting quieter and quieter. I held the phone tight to my ear, wondering if we had a bad connection.

"Sorry, I forgot you don't know everyone. Alex Beekman is new in town, just joined the team—he's an amazing soccer player; the best we've ever had, even if he is gay."

Uncle Gordo didn't say a word. Maybe he wasn't interested, but I felt better talking, so I just barged ahead. "Anyway, Tovitch wants Alex off the team, or at least out of his position. So now he talks as if anyone who even plays to Alex on the field is a fag—"

"Todd." Uncle Gordo's voice was harsh; I caught my breath. "Don't use that word around me."

"Sorry." I untangled myself from the phone. Something cold slid down my spine.

"I think we'd better get something straight," Uncle Gordo said, "although, if I had the choice, I wouldn't do this on the telephone." He paused. "Sometimes I wonder if you know who I am."

I held the phone away from my ear, stared at it a minute, then tucked it back against my head. "Well, of course I do. You're my uncle."

"That's not what I mean." He was quiet a minute, and I couldn't figure out what he was getting at. Was this some kind of game?

Uncle Gordo paused for a long time, then said in a slow, deep voice, "I'm gay, Todd. I'm a gay man. Gary isn't just my business partner; he's also my lover."

Something rang inside my head like a hammer clanging against metal. I leaned against the kitchen cabinet. Everything was falling into place, like marbles tumbling down a narrow chute, gaining momentum as they reached the bottom. I sank to the floor, gripping the phone. I saw Dad cringing when Uncle Gordo reached out to hug him; heard the lame excuses whenever Gordo asked us to come visit and Dad refused. I remembered Dad saying, at the dinner table, *Don't blame me for all your problems*—and the pain in my uncle's eyes.

"Todd?" Uncle Gordo asked gently.

"I didn't know." My voice broke, and I wiped my face with the back of my hand. "No one ever told me."

He groaned. "I'm not surprised—although I always hoped my brother wouldn't pass his prejudices on to you." He laughed, or maybe he was half crying; I couldn't tell. "Homophobia's a national disease; no reason why any of you should be immune."

I closed my eyes, remembering Uncle Gordo's little beach house. The one time we'd visited, a long time ago, Gary was away—and I wondered if that had been planned, to make things easier for Dad. I tried to picture Uncle Gordo there now, standing on his deck with his portable phone in his hand, the wind picking his long hair off his collar, his T-shirt not quite covering his belly. I thought of the Beemer—probably tucked up right next to the house—and the way he'd loaned it to me so easily, his eyes sparkling with delight when he gave me the keys. Something was sliding in and out of my brain, something I didn't understand yet. I kept my eyes closed, hoping I'd get it soon, but it was slippery, like an old rainbow trout in the river. Uncle Gordo's voice brought me back to the room.

"Todd," he said, "do *you* think Alex is gay?"

"I don't know," I mumbled. "Something like this happened to him before, in L.A. I was thinking he might be—but I could be wrong."

"He may not be sure himself," Uncle Gordo said. We were both quiet. I wanted to hang up, but I couldn't. Finally Uncle Gordo said, "If Alex *is* gay, he'll have wild horses galloping around inside his head. It's hard enough to wake up, as a kid, and realize you're different from everyone else. Most of us deny it as long as we can—but our greatest fear is that someone like Tovitch will find out and tell the rest of the world. Believe me, I know just how he feels. Has he made any friends yet?"

"A few," I said, feeling really guilty now. "Two guys on the team—and his twin sister sticks up for him. Molly likes him. . . ." I was sounding lame, and I knew it. I was tempted to say I was Alex's friend too—but Rita was right; I hadn't treated him like one, so there was no point in making myself sound good now.

"It's nice when girls befriend you," Uncle Gordo said, "but it's not the same as having guys who are there when you need them." I heard someone else talking in the background; Uncle Gordo's voice disappeared for a second, then came back. "Sorry—Gary just stepped in. I need to get off in a minute. But tell me—do you think Molly knows about me?"

"I—I'm not sure." I wasn't sure of anything, to tell the truth. The kitchen was spinning. I gripped the leg of a chair next to me, trying to find one spot where I could keep my center of gravity.

"If she doesn't, it might be a good idea to tell her. But she may have figured it out—she's the only one in the family who talks to me much about Gary." Uncle Gordo cleared his throat. "Todd, when life gets confusing— what do you do to feel better?"

"Play soccer," I said immediately. "Or hang out with my friend Sandy—but he's away, unfortunately. And soccer doesn't seem to be such a good place for me anymore."

"How could you make it good again?" Uncle Gordo asked.

"Get Tovitch off the team," I blurted.

Uncle Gordo laughed. "You're joking, right?" he asked. "I doubt that would solve anything."

"Yeah." I shifted the phone to my other ear. My palms were slick and sweaty. Uncle Gordo was right: Tovitch on the sidelines could be even worse than Tovitch on the field. "Actually, the coach benched Tovitch for our scrimmage tomorrow—Randy gave Alex a nasty kick in practice."

"Does the coach know what's going on?" Uncle Gordo asked.

"I'm not sure. Tovitch has always been his pet—he's been getting away with murder until today."

Uncle Gordo cleared his throat. "Sometimes people ignore what they don't want to see. When's your first game?" he asked.

"Friday night at seven, under the lights." I felt groggy and stupid, as if I'd swallowed a sleeping pill. Uncle Gordo's voice was muffled for a second as he talked to Gary. When he came back, he said, "Todd, I've got to go—we've got a major glitch down at the restaurant. I'll share one more thing, and that is: I'm all too familiar with guys like your friend Tovitch. Unfortunately we've got grown-up versions of them here on the Cape. But I have a hunch soccer's the answer for you. Just play the game the way it should be played, and you'll know what to do. You know that Spike Lee movie, what's it called . . ." His voice drifted away, then came back. "Sorry, Nephew—Gary's upset. I need to get off the phone. Don't be afraid to cross the line. Take care—we'll talk again soon. Ciao."

The phone went dead in my hand. I let it fall in my lap. When the line burst into loud angry beeps, I got up, left the receiver dangling, and went to the den, closing the door behind me. I stood at the window, right where Uncle Gordo had been the other night. It had started to rain; the leaves on the lilac bush were slick and shiny. I went to Dad's desk and pulled out the drawers, riffling through old sales slips and canceled checks until I found what I was looking for: a creased Christmas photograph, the kind they make up for you at a camera shop.

I went to the couch and turned on the light, studying the photo. It showed Uncle Gordo and Gary on the deck of their beach house. In the background you could see the dunes and the sharp sea grass bent in the wind. Uncle Gordo's arm was slung over Gary's shoulder. Gary's hair was wild and curly; he was grinning right into the camera, but Gordo's eyes were fixed on Gary, his face lit as if the sun sparkled all over him. I studied the picture for a long time, remembering how, when the card came in the mail last winter, Dad had looked at it once, then shoved it into the drawer instead of setting it on the mantel with the rest of our Christmas cards. I'd been confused then; now I understood.

The kitchen door slammed. I heard the thump of grocery sacks landing heavily on the table and Molly's voice calling, "I'll get the last one." I sank back against the cushions. "Uncle Gordo is gay," I whispered, trying out the words to see how they'd sound, wondering if that would make it real. "My father's own brother is a gay man. And I never knew."

# Chapter Sixteen

The door of the den opened and Molly barged in, her hands full of mail. Her hair was slicked to her head, her T-shirt spotted with raindrops.

"Hi," I said.

Molly yelped, dropping the letters on the floor. "Gee—you could have warned me. Why are you hiding out in here?" She stooped to pick up the envelopes. "Blair's furious. She's gone upstairs looking for you."

I squinted. The room was getting gloomy and dark. "What now?"

"She knows about Friday. Kai's mom was at the market—"

"Damn." I headed for the kitchen, dragging my feet. This was turning into the worst day of my life.

Blair came clattering down the back stairs and nearly fell over me. "Boy, have you got some explaining to do." She glanced at Molly, waving her away. My sister tossed me a pitying look, then disappeared upstairs. I dropped into a chair at the table. Blair stood facing me with her arms crossed, her foot tapping.

"How do you think I feel," she asked in an icy voice, "pushing my cart down the aisle at the Grand Union—when along comes Felicity Stewart, so angry I'm afraid she'll sock me. *Surely* I'll *understand*, Felicity says, why she doesn't want her *darling* Kai to be anywhere near you after what happened Friday night. In fact, she's *so* upset, she sent Kai home early—and she can't help wondering why we never returned her call." Blair took a deep breath. "She and Frank don't see how we can allow you to drive around after you came so close to killing their precious daughter—"

"But no one was hurt!" I protested.

"Todd." Blair's green eyes turned a dark smoky color, always a sign of trouble. "That's hardly the point. You had an accident—and then hid it from us. Did you know Felicity was trying to reach us?"

I shifted uneasily. "Okay, I screwed up. Sorry."

"That's all you have to say?"

I ducked my head. "It wasn't such a big deal—"

Blair slammed the table so hard that jars jangled inside the grocery bags. "Not a big deal! You could have been killed, both of you. And Molly tells me *she* drove you home—which is completely illegal. Then you make up some cock-and-bull story about getting in a fight to explain why your face was black and blue—" she gripped the edge of the table. "Just wait until I get hold of your uncle!"

I stood up fast, knocking over my chair. "Uncle Gordo didn't make me drive that way! It was my fault, and I'm paying for the damages. You're getting everything mixed up. Uncle Gordo loaned me the car *Friday*. My face was smashed up on *Monday*, remember? Randy Tovitch is out to kill me, not that anyone notices—Dad hardly lives here and you're always shut up in the darkroom—"

A dark spot throbbed in the middle of Blair's forehead. "Watch it."

"But it's not fair!" My words came out shaky and broken. "You don't even want to hear *my* side of the story!"

Blair sat down slowly and set her hands on her knees. The old floorboards creaked overhead; Molly's ear was probably glued to the cracks. "All right," Blair said, her voice dead tired. "Start at the beginning."

I paced the room, going through the whole story as fast as possible, toning it down. There was no point in giving her the gory details, such as why I was chasing Randy. I kept it simple, explaining that I was psyched about the Beemer and took Kai for a ride. "I was going too fast," I admitted, "trying to show off. I had a hard time on the curves; I guess I wasn't used to the car."

"Your father was right," Blair said, twisting her hair into a knot. "We should have listened to him. Go on."

Her faced turned white when I described how I came around the last corner. "Randy Tovitch left his truck sitting right on my side of the road," I said. "We would have been okay if he hadn't been such an idiot. I swerved, and did a pretty decent job of missing the trees and making it into Jenson's field—if I do say so."

Blair shook her head. "Don't try to make yourself look good, Todd. It's too late for that now."

"Right." I went on, explaining in a droning voice how we got the car out of the field; how I drove slowly back to Kai's. "It was weird," I said. "I was fine until the Stewarts' house. But then I got the shakes and threw up in the bushes. I figured we'd be safer if Molly drove home. She did a good job, too," I added.

Blair was quiet for a long time. "Let's be honest here," she said at last. "What *should* you have done?"

"Called you," I said, because I knew that's what she wanted to hear. Of course, it had never crossed my mind.

Blair went to the sink, drank a glass of water, then leaned against the counter. "You could have been killed." She was almost whispering, and the house was so still, each creak resounded like a firecracker.

"I told you, I'm sorry—"

" 'Sorry' is too late, if you hurt someone."

"But I didn't!" I cried, yelling now. "And the car was barely scratched! Plus, I grounded myself, if you'd like to know!"

She cocked her head. "Explain, please."

"Remember last weekend, how I never went anywhere? And now I'm only using the car to get to practice and back."

"Whose idea was that?" she asked. "Yours—or Gordon's?"

"I guess—we figured it out together."

"I see." Her eyes stayed steady on my face. "So you're in cahoots with your uncle. How long were you planning to hide this from us?"

"It was between me and him," I said. When she put her

hands on her hips, I protested, "That's what *you* said, Blair! When Dad didn't want me to drive the BMW, you told him it was between me and Uncle Gordo!"

"That hardly applies to this situation." Blair pushed her hair back from her face. "You should be grounded at least until school starts. I'll have to discuss it with Mark."

I picked up a jar of pickles, rolling it between my hands. "Couldn't you tell him after our first game?"

Blair rummaged in her garden basket and pulled out an onion. "Are you afraid Mark will keep you from playing?"

"Sort of," I said. "And if he screams and yells at me, I'll probably screw up. Things on the team are pretty crazy as it is." My eyes filled again; I looked away.

Blair came over to me, her hands resting gently on my shoulders. "You say I don't notice anything. But I've been watching. You're a different person since the season started," she said. "What's the matter?"

"I can't explain," I said. "It's too complicated."

Blair sighed and went to the sink, pulling a knife from the dish rack. She sliced an onion with quick, angry strokes. "So the game's more important than being open with Mark?"

I glared at her. "*You* should talk about being open."

Blair froze, her hand poised. "What does that mean?"

"How come you and Dad never told us about Uncle Gordo?"

"What?" Blair dropped the knife. It bounced on the counter and clattered to the floor. "Damn—I've cut myself." She held her finger under cold water, glancing at me sideways. "Uncle Gordo? What are you talking about?"

I circled the table, pushing chairs in, yanking them out. "You know what I mean! Uncle Gordo is gay! Why didn't you tell me!"

Blair slumped into a chair, holding a dish towel to her finger. "I couldn't," she whispered, biting her lip. "Not without Mark's permission. Believe me, Todd, I tried to change his mind—"

"You should have tried harder!" I yelled. "Because now it's too late, and everything's screwed up! Do you understand? It's ruining the team!"

Blair's face puckered. "Todd, what on earth does Uncle Gordo being gay have to do with playing soccer?"

"You wouldn't understand; not in a million years." I went to the door, opened it, and stood there a second, glaring at her through my tears. "That's why we never go visit him, isn't it? You're ashamed, and so is Dad. I saw the way he won't even hug Uncle Gordo. He's embarrassed by his own brother."

"Todd, wait—" Blair dropped the dish towel and reached for me. But I was gone, skidding down the steps and across the driveway. The sharp stones stung my bare feet; I ran at the edge of the field, the tall grass wetting my ankles, until I reached the electric fence. I jumped over it, retrieved my ball, and vaulted out again. My right hand touched the wire, giving me a nasty shock, but I kept going, kicking the ball in front of me as I ducked into the woods. I jogged along the path beside the river, shaking my hand to numb the pain.

I ran hard, panting and choking as I stubbed my toes on stumps and heavy stones. I went past the spot where I'd talked with Rita, past the tree house I'd built with

Sandy, following the narrow, overgrown trail until I came to the big hemlock that hung over the river, its feathery needles trailing into the water like fingers.

I stooped to get in under the branches, let the ball bounce on the soft needles, and crawled on my hands and knees to my mom's stone. The rough piece of quartz glistened in the rain. I ran my hands over the plaque, feeling the raised letters of my mother's name: Ashley Bell O'Connor. "Ashley," I whispered, and sank onto the carpet of pine needles, my head pounding. "What am I supposed to do now?" A tiny wind ruffled the branches and the river trickled past, but there was no response from my mother—or anyone else.

"What the hell is going on!" My voice cut through the dark. I lay flat, letting the rain wash my face, wishing the night could swallow me up and take me far away.

It was almost dark when I heard footsteps, then Molly's voice calling softly, "Todd? Where are you?"

I sat up. "In here," I muttered as her bare legs flashed by. She stopped, parted the branches, and came in with me, pushing back the hood of her raincoat. With her hair pulled tight in its short braid, her face looked hollow and bony.

"You're just sitting here in the rain?" Molly said.

I shrugged; I hadn't really noticed.

She sat close to me. "How'd you find out about Uncle Gordo?" she asked.

"He told me on the phone."

Molly leaned against me. "I guessed when he was here," she said, "but I wasn't sure. It was the way Uncle

Gordo talked about Gary, like—well, you know, like they're a couple."

"They are." The idea still made me feel strange and prickly, as if I were swimming in a lake full of hidden leeches. "It just seems so weird," I said.

"To you," Molly said, "but not to them."

"And to Dad, obviously," I said. "Do you think that's why he wouldn't tell us?"

Molly scooped some pine needles into a mound. "Who knows? He's pretty prejudiced about some things. It explains a lot, though, doesn't it?"

"You mean, how awkward he and Gordo are together?" I asked, and Molly nodded. "You'd think he'd be more accepting of his own brother."

Molly gave me one of her piercing looks. "You should talk."

"About what?" I demanded.

"About being accepting," she said. "You're not very nice to Alex, you know."

I winced, glad she couldn't see my face. "Alex is all right," I mumbled.

Molly's fingernails made deep tracks in the needles. "So how come you make fun of him—along with everyone else?"

"I don't," I said. "It's just—" I hesitated, but Molly's gray eyes, so steady and fierce, made me finish. "Damn it, Mol! According to Tovitch, anyone who even *looks* at Alex is a fag. Randy's made everything ugly!"

"So that's what you and Randy fought about?"

"Part of it," I said.

"Randy's a jerk," Molly said, waving her hand as if she

could brush him away. "But what if Alex *is* gay? So what?"

I held onto my knees. "Being gay is weird, Mol."

"To you, maybe," she said quietly. "I think it's just another way to be." When I didn't answer, she added, "Anyway, if Alex is weird, then Uncle Gordo must be too."

There it was: the slippery thing I'd tried to take hold of when I was talking to Uncle Gordo on the phone. I held my head in my hands, thinking of my uncle's belly laugh, the way he'd trusted me with his new car. There was no way I'd ever call him weird. Crazy, sure, but he was Uncle Gordo, the one we'd always loved. "This is giving me a massive headache," I told Molly.

She was quiet a minute; then she said, "Alex thinks you hate him."

I peered at her, trying to get a clear view of her eyes. "How do you know?"

"He told me."

What was this, the day of a zillion surprises? "Since when are you and Alex big buddies?"

"Since— I don't know." She pulled up her hood. It was raining harder now. "Since Kai's party, I guess. We have a lot in common. Friends we miss in California. And also, Alex and I are both odd." She said it in the same matter-of-fact way Alex had used when he was talking about Molly in our kitchen. She's right, I thought; they are kind of alike.

"Well, isn't that nice?" I said, balancing on my heels. "I'm so glad you know Beekman's darkest secrets."

"You've heard some of them too," Molly said quietly.

I squirmed and turned away. "I don't know everything about him," Molly went on, "but I guess Rita does. They can read each other's mind; did you know that?"

"Yeah, I've seen it in action."

Molly gave me a half smile. "Good thing we can't do that."

"Really. Tell me about it."

She stood up, stooping to fit under the branches. Her face got sad again. "It's so awful for Alex, Todd. Can't you make the guys quit baiting him?"

I jumped to my feet and hurled my ball against the tree. It bounced away into the woods. "You've got no idea what it's like, dealing with Tovitch!" I cried.

Molly shrugged. "Randy's just trying to be macho," she said. "He's probably a wimp underneath. Why should he run everything?"

I didn't have an answer for that one. "Come up for dinner, okay?" Molly said, and took off. The hemlock branches scratched her yellow slicker as she ducked onto the trail. My teeth chattered; the rain had soaked my shirt and tangled my hair against my scalp. Randy, a wimp? Give me a break.

I knocked through the bushes until I found my ball. A comment of Uncle Gordo's still tugged at me: something about the title of a Spike Lee movie. Damn. Why couldn't I remember what he'd said?

I touched my mother's stone one more time, but the answer didn't come. I left her grave, stumbled along the wet, dark path, and dragged my feet up the driveway to the house, clutching my soccer ball under my arm. It seemed like the last steady thing in my life.

# Chapter Seventeen

Tovitch was right. We didn't do so hot in the scrimmage without him, but we didn't lose either. We finished with a tie; Drew scored our only goal. Alex came in and out; his charley horse still hurt. As for Tovitch, he was barely on the bench. He leaned toward the field as if someone held him back with a rope, his legs bouncing up and down, eyes spitting at Alex. Every time we made a bad play, Tovitch swore, until Crawford threatened to send him home.

After the game I went straight for my car, even though I could have used a shower. Blair was only allowing me to drive to practice and back, so I had to get away fast, but Crawford called me over to help him load the gear into his van.

"Good playing," the coach said, as I hoisted the big water jug into the back. "You okay at midfield?"

"It's all right," I said, hedging.

"Front-line glamour isn't everything," Crawford said. "No one notices Craig at sweeper—until they realize he stops every ball that comes his way. We need someone steady at midfield, too."

I smiled. Crawford had a backhanded way of giving compliments, but it still felt good. The long yellow bus full of our opponents belched exhaust as it lurched out of the parking lot. I held my breath, then let it out slow. "Coach," I said.

He paused, halfway into his van. "Shoot."

My palms were sweaty. Why was this so hard? "Coach, I know this is none of my business—but why don't you leave Tovitch at striker? He's more aggressive than Alex—and Beekman's good at those long passes from the wing—" Crawford's face didn't even twitch; I kept going. "I thought maybe if you switched them, Tovitch wouldn't be so pissed, that's all."

Crawford gave me a cool nod. "You're right, Todd; it is none of your business. Still, I appreciate the suggestion, and I'll certainly think about it when I make my final decision." He slid into his seat, slammed the door, and drove away.

Hard-ass, I thought. Well, I'd tried. Now there was nothing more to do.

It poured all day Thursday, soaking the field. We did boring drills in the gym with the junior varsity, then watched videos of the U.S. men's soccer team.

"Listen," Crawford said, hitting the pause button again and again. "Hear the way these pros talk to each other before they pass? All the way down the field? I expect that kind of talk between you guys tomorrow night."

After Crawford finished trying to pump us up, I ran downstairs. Alex was already outside, holding his bag. The rain had plastered his hair to his head; his shell clung to his T-shirt. He turned away when he saw me.

"Sorry I can't give you a ride," I said, trying to sound friendly. "I have to bring the Subaru straight home. Blair found out about my accident, so I'm grounded." Of course, Blair probably wouldn't mind if I went by the Beekmans'. But Alex just shrugged and said, "I'm all set."

Craig came out, splashing through deep puddles, and motioned Alex to his car without looking at me. Obviously they'd planned this ahead of time. My face burned. I turned away and stowed my gear in the Subaru. For some reason the thought of Craig and Alex hanging out together made me even more depressed. I sat in my car, watching Craig's beat-up sedan pull out into traffic. When his tail lights disappeared around the corner, I backed out slowly. I didn't want to follow them too closely.

I shoved a Marley tape into the player. The sound blasted through the car, but even so the Subaru still felt empty. "Please," I whispered to no one in particular, "let the game fix everything." Even though it was impossible for anyone to grant me that wish, I could still hope—couldn't I?

Friday evening Blair dropped me at the high school an hour before the game. Things hadn't been too good between us the last few days, but she seemed willing to forget it. "Have fun," she said as I stepped out of the car. "Molly and I will be here at seven o'clock sharp."

"Thanks," I said. Of course, I'd be lucky if I could even move. My stomach was in knots, my legs were killing me, and I had to take a leak again, even though I'd been twice before we left the house.

As we suited up in the locker room, I remembered the games I'd subbed in last year, when the varsity players strutted around half dressed, giving each other playful punches, getting pumped up. Tonight everyone seemed to be avoiding eye contact, and each time a locker opened, the clang of metal echoed through the room.

Suddenly the coach flung the door open. He stood there a second, taking us in. His face was flushed and his eyes sparkled, as if he were ready to go out on the field himself. "Someone die?" he demanded. No one answered. Crawford hopped up on a bench so he could see everyone. "Where's your spirit? Let's show a little enthusiasm. What are we going to do tonight?"

"Kick butt!" a couple of guys shouted, and the rest of us muttered, "Go Griswold."

"Not very convincing." Crawford waited for a more rousing cheer and, when nothing happened, rubbed his mustache, looked down at his clipboard, and said, "All right, here's the starting lineup."

Now we were *really* quiet. "Alex, stay at center, where you played yesterday. Randy, left wing; Drew on the right." He glanced at me. "Todd, center mid; Dex, right midfield, Benji, left . . . Craig at sweeper; you'll mark Schofield, Midland's top player. . . . He's a tall redhead; you can't miss him."

Crawford went on with the rest of the defense, but I was too nervous to pay attention. I glanced at Tovitch.

His face was dark and shadowy as he pulled socks on over his shin guards. Rich, Dex, and Benji muttered together. And Beekman stood by the window, suited and ready, his face shut like a door that's been slammed hard. I shivered. What would happen on the field?

"Play your hearts out," Crawford said. We burst from the locker room in a tight bunch, jostling each other. Even though there were guys all around, I felt lonely as hell.

We stretched and jogged in place, warming up. "O'Connor." Tovitch grabbed a ball and gave it an easy kick. I trapped it and passed back, on my guard. What could he want? He dribbled it over to me, flashing his chipped-tooth grin as though we were best buddies now.

"This is it, O'Connor," he said. "The night we show our stuff. Crawford can give away my position, but he can't control the way we play the game."

I forced myself to look into his eyes. The black pupils merged with the irises, making them seem bigger and darker than usual. "What did you have in mind?" I asked carefully, returning the ball.

"I mean, you pass to me, on the wing, as often as you can—"

"Of course," I said. "That's part of our strategy, getting the ball to you—"

He nodded. "Yeah, but I'm talking about more than that. If we keep the ball away from Alex, he won't be able to score. Then I can get my striker position back— and maybe you'll be on the forward line, where you belong." He picked the ball up and threw it in the air. I met it with my forehead, knocking it back, and was about to turn away when he added, "Plus, we can show Beekman that fags don't belong on this team."

I drew back. That word seemed ugly now, with raw, cutting edges. "I'm just planning to play soccer—and win," I said. "You'd better do the same."

"Fag lover," Randy muttered, but I managed to ignore him for once.

For the next few minutes Drew and I helped Ozzie warm up. We took turns feeding him short, hard passes, always aiming for the far corners of the net. Ozzie was good; neither one of us got a shot past him. Pretty soon, I started to calm down. The fans drifted in, and the Midland team spread out across the far end of the field.

"Those guys have got some size on them," Drew said. Of course he'd notice that, being the shortest starter.

"Yeah," I said. "Midland doesn't play football anymore. Maybe that's why they've got so many fans here." In fact, our own crowd looked decent too; it was the first home game of the season.

Just then Molly and Rita cruised past on their way to the bleachers. My sister waved, but Rita acted as if I didn't exist, saving her most dazzling smile for Craig. Then she raised her eyebrows at Alex, and I knew they were sharing a secret signal. Alex did a little warm-up dance, bouncing from one foot to the other.

I remembered the Beekmans' first day in town; how Rita gave *me* one of her famous smiles when we met. Now I'd disappeared, as far as she was concerned. I retrieved the ball from the sidelines and kicked it as hard as I could at Ozzie. To my surprise, it sailed right past him.

"Glad you're not on the Midland team," Ozzie said, grunting as he picked himself up.

"I just caught you off guard," I said and grinned, promising to make that same kick when the game started. The Midland goalie would miss it by a mile, the team would work together, right? Wrong, O'Connor. Dream on.

But then something amazing happened. The sun went down just as the lights came up, so the last of the daylight seemed to bleed into the flickering glow of the halogens. I stood still, my heart beating fast. For years I'd been watching other varsity players warm up on this field, their green shorts matching the clean-cut grass, their white jerseys glowing eerily in the artificial light. But I'd never realized what a surge I'd get when the cheers and whistles were for me and my team. I wanted to dance and strut, to kick the ball to the far end of the field. "Go Griswold!" I shouted, surprising myself. "Let's win!"

"Yeah!" Craig answered from across the field, and for the first time in days he smiled at me, raising his fist in a salute.

The ref blew a whistle, drawing both teams to the center of the field. We knelt in semicircles, facing each other, raising the soles of our cleats so the ref could check for metal spikes. "Any jewelry, watches, leave them on the sidelines," he said. The other referee took the two captains aside and tossed the coin.

"Looks like we won the toss," Drew said, nudging me. Sure enough, Ozzie was grinning; he pointed to the field, choosing to defend first.

"Take your positions!" Crawford crouched on one knee

like a runner before a dash. The subs ran to the bench, and I jogged to the midfield, scanning the opposing team as they passed. I remembered Schofield from last year: a tall, lanky kid with a carrot head and even more freckles than me; he was playing opposite Alex. On an impulse I jogged to the center line and said to Beekman, under my breath, "Watch your opposite—lead scorer last year. He's known for fouls."

Alex whirled around. "Thanks," he said. "Not to worry." He looked different tonight. His eyes were bright, and he tossed his hair off his forehead like a colt ready for the races, his cheeks flushed a bright pink. "Just pass the ball forward, we'll take care of it," he said, jogging in place.

Randy called out, "Yeah, send it to the wings." He bounced outside the center circle, his sturdy legs pumping. Alex fixed his eyes on the ball. I tried to swallow the tension erupting in my gut. The whistle blew, Schofield and another forward gave the ball a couple of short, quick kicks, and the game began.

It took the Midland guys about two minutes to realize Beekman was a major problem. Whenever Alex got control of the ball, the Midland coach yelled at his defense, "Get that guy! Keep it away from him!"

Alex was everywhere, managing to stay clear for passes —except they didn't always come his way. Tovitch obviously had Dex and other defensive guys in on his scheme, because no matter how open Alex was, the ball kept going out to the wings, leaving him high and dry. Only Craig and Drew passed to him consistently, and the same conspiracy kept the ball away from me. The coach yelled his head off on the sidelines, but I was too fixed on the game to pay much attention. Every time I got halfway down the field, the play changed direction and I had to spin and run the other way.

Finally Craig passed me the ball. I stopped it, glancing up. Alex was out in the open, with a beautiful clean stretch of field behind him. "Todd, here!" he called, waving his long arm.

"Out to the *wing!*" Tovitch shouted. I hesitated and in that split second lost the ball. Schofield came out of nowhere and snagged it from me, barreling down the center. He was faster than any of us. He passed off to the side, got himself clear, and was ready when the wing sent it back in. I lunged but missed. Schofield made a short, choppy kick, sending the ball right over Ozzie's outstretched hands into the soft scoop of the net.

A goal! I groaned as the buzzer sounded. The opposing fans went wild, and the Midland guys practically danced up the field, jumping in the air to give each other high fives.

I jogged slowly back to midline. Alex was waiting for me, his eyes blazing, his face dead white. "What's wrong with you?" he demanded. "Didn't you see I was out there all alone? You practically gave it away."

"Sorry." He was right, of course. I clamped my lips together and took my position again. For the next few minutes we formed a straight attack on the Midland goal. Alex dribbled down the center, passed off to Drew, then positioned himself for a return kick. But when Drew got rid of it, Tovitch charged in front of Alex, just the way he'd played it Tuesday. Damn; was he trying to disable Beekman again? The Midland goalie scooped up the ball and sent it back out into play before I even had time to reach the penalty box. When a Midland player kicked the ball over the line, the horn blew for subs and a hand clapped my shoulder.

"You're out, O'Connor." I stared. It was Phil, a kid who could barely play. What was going on? "Off the field," the ref snapped at me.

I jogged to the bench. "O'Connor," the coach called, his eyes glued to the game, "Alex could have scored if you'd passed it to him. I hope that wasn't intentional."

"What about Tovitch?" I protested. "He's blatant!"

"Just take care of yourself," Crawford said. I thought about Tovitch boasting that the coach would never take *him* off the field and went for water, fuming.

I'd downed four cups before I happened to glance at the parking lot. I blinked twice and rubbed my eyes, edging closer to the fence. Uncle Gordo's BMW, still boasting its long scratch on the door, was sitting in the lot, its hood gleaming in the lights.

"What the—" I scanned the crowd on the bleachers, then stood back so I could see the long line of people clustered beside the rope. It only took me a few seconds to find Uncle Gordo; he was taller and more solid than most of the fans. He stood apart from the crowd, rocking back and forth on his toes. I stared. Something hot and liquid boiled up in my chest as I watched him, my mouth open. Uncle Gordo was completely into the game. He leaned toward the field, shouting and waving his arms when someone made a good play. His hair was pulled back into a scruffy ponytail, and he was wearing a beat-up leather jacket. He looked like someone from a tough motorcycle gang.

My eyes smarted. I swiped them quickly with the sleeve of my jersey. Why had he come to my game?

"Send it to Beekman!" Crawford called just as Uncle Gordo shouted, "Pass to number ten!" I snapped my head back toward the field. Alex, in the number-ten jersey, was perfectly positioned in front of the goal, but Randy ignored him. Instead he took a shot from too far out, missing the post by a mile.

"Don't hog the ball!" Uncle Gordo yelled. He turned, spotted me and waved, beaming.

I waved back. My head throbbed, and I panted for breath as if I were back on the field. I hurried over to Crawford, who paced up and down the line, screeching, "Pass it to Beekman, you jerks! He's in position to score!"

"Coach," I said, tagging along behind him. "Send me back in. *I'll* help Alex score—I promise." Crawford gave me a quick, vague look, then swung back to the game.

"Please," I begged. "Give me another chance."

My voice cracked, and this time Crawford snapped his head around to look at me. "All right—but don't blow it again," he said, and called to the ref, "Substitution."

I danced at the center line, trying to stay warm, waiting my turn. It came in less than a minute. As I ran onto the field, someone called, "Come on, Griswold, score!" It was Uncle Gordo, his deep voice booming above the crowd.

Okay, I thought, finding a new surge of energy. I tapped Phil, sent him to the bench, and waited for the whistle to blow. When it did, I exploded into play, my legs churning, my whole body aimed for the ball. Midland had control, but Craig made a beautiful save outside the penalty box, trapped it and sent it up to me. In that split second before my left foot smacked leather, the title of Spike Lee's movie flashed across my brain, the words shimmering like the bright numbers on our scoreboard: *Do the right thing.*

Without hesitating I trapped the ball and passed it straight to Alex. He was waiting, out in the open, his eyes intent and watchful, his body poised to receive the ball—as if we'd planned it that way all along.

# Chapter Eighteen

For the next few minutes we managed to keep control of the ball. Alex dribbled a few yards, dodged a defender, and passed off to Drew, who took it down the line, then sent it back to me as the Midland defense closed in.

"Out to the wing!" Tovitch screamed. He was heavily guarded, so I kept running, dodging the Midland stopper. I was about to take a shot on goal myself when someone screamed "Man on!" and Alex suddenly appeared to my left.

"Pass it forward," Beekman called, his voice steady and calm as the defenders charged. I managed a short, choppy pass just before the Midland sweeper scrambled for my feet. Randy ran to intercept it, but Beekman was there first. Alex stopped the ball with his right knee and let it roll down his leg as casually as if he had all the time in the world. He glanced up once, his eyes flickering as he spotted the keeper's position, then made a beautiful, left-footed shot that sailed into the far corner of the net. The Midland goalie never had a chance.

Our fans roared. "Goal for Griswold by Beekman, assist, O'Connor," the loudspeaker blared. Alex didn't smile, but his eyes danced as he slapped my hand. "Beautiful assist!" he said.

"Way to score!" Drew pounded our backs. Craig ran forward to greet us with high fives as we bounced to the center line. The defense congratulated each other, and even Dex yelled, "Nice goal, Beekman!" But Randy's face was contorted, and he was royally pissed when Crawford yelled, "Tovitch, off the field! Todd, play left wing."

I whirled around, wondering if I'd heard right. "Go on, move up," Crawford ordered, waving me forward. He tapped Phil for my midfield position. We got in line for the Midland kick-off, and Tovitch paced in a tight circle near the bench, digging into the grass with the heel of his shoe while Crawford chewed him out.

The whistle blew and Uncle Gordo's voice boomed, "Go, Todd! Come on, Griswold, score again!"

I still couldn't get over Uncle Gordo coming to my game. But there wasn't time to think about why he was there. Now that the score was tied, Midland was pushing for another goal. We had a tough fight on our hands, and the clock was ticking down the half. We got close to the Midland goal a few times, but they always drove us back. I got called for offsides, which gave Midland a kick, then Dexter let the ball go right by him. Schofield took control, ran flat out down the center of the field, and sent the ball into the net with a powerhouse kick that left Ozzie lying flat.

The Midland fans went bananas, and Ozzie pounded

the ground with his fist. Two minutes later the buzzer sounded for the end of the half. Were we jinxed without Tovitch?

Alex limped off the field ahead of me. "Put some ice on that leg," Crawford told him, opening the first-aid box. He seemed to know I was there without even turning his head. "O'Connor, you know better than to get called for offsides."

"Sorry." I caught up to Craig, on his way to the locker room. "I hate switching positions like that, in the middle of the game," I said. "Gets me confused."

"Yeah," Craig said, breathing hard and fast. "We need you at midfield. Should have stopped that last goal." He stopped to catch his breath. "What's Crawford up to?"

"Who knows? After practice yesterday, I suggested he put Randy back at striker. He told me to mind my own business."

"Too bad," Craig said. "It's late for changes like that now." We stopped at the water fountain outside the door. My lungs were burning up. I leaned against the brick wall, feeling wasted. Craig wiped his mouth and stepped aside to let me drink. "Keep sending them up to Alex; we'll have it made."

"Hope so," I said.

We went into the locker room. It was a zoo in there. Guys were groaning, taping their sore ankles, yelling over the slamming of locker doors. I dodged a towel that came flying my way and headed for my locker. Tovitch sat on the bench in the middle of it all, knees spread wide, a big grin on his face.

"What's so funny?" I asked.

"*You* guys," he said. "Playing up to the fag—why don't you bring Midland their goal on a silver platter next time, dish it up nice and easy?"

The pressure suddenly burst in my chest. I lunged at Tovitch, grabbing his shoulders. "Stop using that word!" I screamed, shaking him so hard his head knocked against the metal locker. Hands grabbed us from every side.

"Cool it!" Ozzie yelled, pushing me away. "Leave this stuff, will you?" I stumbled backward. Tovitch rubbed the back of his head.

"What's going on here?" Crawford's voice cut through the racket.

I straightened up, still gulping for breath. "Tell him to stop the name calling!" I yelled, pointing at Tovitch.

Crawford stalked toward us, hands on his hips. "Didn't I warn you to leave your petty fights at home? Stuff it, both of you. We don't have time for this crap now. If you want to play, listen to me. We've got a tough fight ahead."

I took long slow breaths. My heart was hopping around inside my chest.

Crawford glared at Tovitch, then me, before turning to everyone else. "Listen up!" When the noise settled a little, he said, "Here's the strategy for the next half—"

"Wait a minute," I said, stepping so close my chin almost touched Crawford's; I could smell his hot breath. "If Tovitch called Craig a nigger, would you ignore it?"

The silence was so sudden, I could hear the steady drip of water in the tiled shower room. My voice didn't come out right; my throat felt coated with sandpaper.

"Of course not," Crawford said. His feet were planted wide. He held his ground.

"But 'fag' is all right?" I said. "Tovitch can strut up and down calling Beekman a fag, and you could care less." Too late I realized Alex was frozen in the doorway, half in, half out.

I waited for the coach to say something. Finally Crawford cleared his throat. Two red spots burned on his cheekbones. "I don't stand for any name calling on this team," he said. "You know that."

His eyes wouldn't meet mine, and suddenly I recognized Crawford's expression. Sure, he had a man's face; his eyes were that steel-blue instead of rusty-brown— but I saw myself there just the same, the guy I was before Uncle Gordo called: afraid and shifty—the self I could still be, if I didn't watch out. My knees wobbled, and I dropped to the bench.

"If you don't allow it, Coach, why don't you stop it?" Drew asked. He stood in front of Alex like a small shield, quivering. Tension crackled in the room. I remembered what Uncle Gordo had said: that people ignore what they don't want to see. Crawford's known all along, I thought. He's as bad as the rest of us, as bad as my dad—or me.

Finally Ozzie broke the silence. "O'Connor's right, Coach. There's a lot of ugly stuff going on. We need to talk about it sometime. But right now we've got to win this game. Only a few minutes left until the second half." He pulled on his gloves. "Face it—Tovitch is keeping the ball from Beekman; Dex, Rich, and Benji are working with him. Long as that happens, we don't have a chance."

"Ozzie's right, Coach," Craig said. "There's a lot of ball hogging, not enough passing, like you said in practice."

Crawford blinked and looked down at his clipboard as if trying to remember where all this started. Tovitch stood up and glanced around the room, his eyes searching for his cohorts. Rich turned away, and even Dex muttered, "Let's lay off, Tove."

Tovitch picked up his jacket and slid his arms slowly into one sleeve, then the other. "I get the message," he said. "I'm out of here."

Crawford whacked his clipboard against a locker. "What the hell! You can't just ditch the team!"

"I can if I want." Tovitch stuck his chin out, but his eyes had the same soft, hurt look as when he was cleaning up his wounded horse. What had Molly said? *He's probably a wimp underneath.* Not a wimp, I thought. But afraid of a few things. His dad, for one. Feeling cornered, the way he is now, for another.

"Don't be a jerk, Tovitch." We turned to the door. Alex still leaned against the frame, his hand holding the ice pack against his thigh. "You can't cut out on us now," he said, his voice shaking. "We need you to win this thing."

Tovitch seemed poised on the balls of his feet, like he didn't know which way to run. "Yeah," I said to his back. "Aren't you hungry for a goal? I am."

Tovitch didn't answer, but his hunched shoulders relaxed a little.

"You're not leaving," Crawford said. His voice was tired, as if he'd run every play of the game with us. "That's an order." Their eyes met for a second, and then the coach studied his clipboard. "Let's try you back at striker," he said easily, as if the last few minutes had never happened. I took a couple of long, slow breaths.

"So, Tovitch gets what he wants," Craig muttered in my ear, but I raised my hand to shut him up. Crawford's doing what I suggested, I thought. He listened to me after all. I held my head in my hands so the coach couldn't see my sloppy grin.

"O'Connor, go back to center mid; we'll have Beekman at left wing; everyone else as before."

Alex gave me a weak smile. "Sounds good. Not to brag, but I play better out there. And Tovitch should be the striker; he's more aggressive—"

"You can say *that* again," Drew broke in, and the room exploded with nervous laughter.

"Shut up!" Crawford snapped, but it was too late; he'd lost our attention. Two little sparks flickered in Randy's eyes. He stripped off his jacket and tossed it on the floor, a good sign.

"Time, Coach," Ozzie yelled over the racket. Crawford clapped his hands hard and we half listened while he pumped us up with a list of quick orders. "Let's win!" Craig yelled, and the rest of us let fly with cheers and whistles, answered by a roar from our fans as we burst through the door onto the field.

# Chapter Nineteen

As we jogged past the stands, I scanned the crowd for Uncle Gordo. He clasped his hands over his head when I waved to him. "Two more like the last one!" he called.

Craig pulled my shoulder. "Good stuff," he said. I grinned my thanks and beckoned to Alex, who was waiting for me near the bench.

"Hey, I've got an idea," I told Beekman, but he wasn't listening. He stuck out his right hand and shook mine as if we'd just met for the first time.

"Thanks," he said gruffly. He tossed his hair back and went out onto the field.

"Wait," I said, following him. "Beekman, hold on." I beckoned to Tovitch and Drew. "Can you guys come over here?"

We grouped near the center line. Drew and Alex looked wary. "What's up?" Tovitch asked, keeping his distance.

"Let's try that crossover maneuver the coach taught us last week," I said. Randy's eyes flickered with interest as

I explained. "Alex or Drew fake it. They run across the field, leap over the ball and keep going. I pick it up from behind, send it to Tovitch—"

"And I score," Tovitch said, punching his open palm. "Excellent."

"Thirty seconds!" the ref called. We ran for our positions, and the second half began.

Midland's defense was confused when they found Alex and Randy in different spots. For the first ten minutes the ball went up and down the field, running our midfield—meaning me—completely ragged. Then Craig managed to snag the ball from Schofield and send it to me. That was my chance.

"Beekman!" I yelled, and passed to the left side. Alex was right on it. He ran straight across the field, rather than toward the goal. With a dancer's graceful leap, he jumped the ball and kept going in a perfect fake, leaving it to me. Tovitch surged into the empty spot Alex had left behind and was there to intercept the ball when I passed it forward. The Midland defense was screwed up now. Their goalie had come too far out of the goal box, giving Tovitch a clear shot, which he took—and won.

"Score!" I yelled, twirling in midair. The crowd went nuts; we were tied up again. I jumped my way back to the midline, grinning, punching everyone. "Goal, Tovitch; assist, O'Connor," the loudspeaker boomed. Randy ran to the center with his arms held high. All the defensive men ran up to congratulate him, and Alex called out, "Nice shot!"

"Thinks he's won the Olympics," Craig said, slapping my back. "Never mind—that was brilliant. Two assists—way to go."

"Thanks," I said, jogging in place. "Just keep sending them up to us—you're doing great, Craig. Go Griswold!" I yelled, and from the sidelines, clear as anything, Uncle Gordo's hoarse voice answered, "Do it again!"

But Midland wasn't about to make it easy. Their coach, a pot-bellied guy who looked like he hadn't run anywhere in ten years, was having fits on the sideline. "Get number ten!" he screeched, and Schofield actually clipped Alex once or twice without the ref noticing. "Foul!" Crawford screamed, but no whistle blew and we kept playing. We tried the crossover twice more, but Midland caught on fast, so we fought it out up and down the field, with Craig, Rich, and Ozzie making some amazing saves. The coach pulled us out, one at a time, for drinks of water and short rests, then sent us back in. "Five minutes left!" Crawford yelled when Drew returned to the field, the last starter to get a break. "Give it everything you've got!"

The score was still tied up when Schofield gave us an opening. Alex had maneuvered the ball close to the penalty line and was about to pass to Randy when the big redhead charged Tovitch. Before the ball even left Alex's foot, Randy was down. This time it was too obvious for the ref to ignore. His whistle shrieked. Tovitch writhed on the ground, then exploded to his feet, ready to fight.

"Steady," Alex warned, grabbing Randy's arm.

"Don't touch me," Tovitch snarled, but Alex kept his hold.

"Indirect kick!" the ref announced.

"Give that guy a yellow card!" Crawford screeched from the sidelines as the ref set the ball in place.

"Tovitch," I whispered, catching hold of his other arm.

"Get your hands off me, you—" he gulped, but caught himself, seeing the ref's face. Swearing would give Tovitch his own penalty.

"Listen," I said, twisting his shirt in my fist. "When you take the kick, I'll come up from behind and run to the right. Make believe you're going to pass to me—"

Randy's eyes narrowed to slits; he almost smiled. "But send it to Beekman instead." Then he scowled, realizing what he'd have to do.

"Come *on*," I urged. "It's our chance to win."

"I'll see," he said, twisting away from me.

The whistle sounded. Tovitch took his slow steps back in preparation for the kick. Midland's defense, huddled in a line to protect their goal, broke in my direction as I bolted. Tovitch ran for the ball, turned his body as if to kick to me—then spun a hundred and eighty degrees and sent the ball right into the empty spot the defense had left for Alex. Randy's kick was strong and direct. Beekman stopped the ball with his chest, ran with it a few steps, and shot it high, just over the goalie's head. It nicked the crossbar—and swished into the net.

"All right!" I yelled, punching the air.

"Goal, Beekman; assist, Tovitch," the loudspeaker blared. "Ten . . . nine . . . eight . . ." the crowd roared, counting down the final seconds.

Tovitch spun in the air, and I almost fell over, laughing. He'd given the ball to Beekman—and together they'd won the game.

*Afterward I always wished I'd had a videotape of those last few minutes. I wanted to hold a remote in my hand, hitting the pause button at that final moment, just so I could see the expression on Tovitch's face. If Crawford had been in charge of the controls, he'd say, "See? Watch this move, in slow motion. Alex is perfectly positioned, and Tovitch has set it up just right. Todd starts to run, fooling the defense—allowing Tovitch to pass to Alex, who sends it into the goal."*

*I'd hold it right there. The audience might watch the ball, its sweet curve into the net, or agonize with the Midland keeper, his face contorted as he realizes he can't prevent the goal. But my eyes would be glued to Randy's face—to the slow burn that explodes—not into flames, as I might have thought, but into something else—confusion, puzzlement, pleasure in spite of himself—because you can't make an assist that wins a game and not be happy about it. Even if you're Randy Tovitch. And I know, watching him, that he'll never really change—but that something will be different after this.*

*As guys surround Tovitch, pounding his back, congratulating him, the camera pans to Alex. I'd pause again, holding it on Rich and Dex and Benji as they give Alex grudging high fives before they take off to greet their friends. I'd stick with Beekman, zooming in on his long fingers, which twist the silver ring around* and around, the spinning of the ring reminding me that he's made the goal for someone far away. His face is brighter than the lamps overhead; his eyes search the crowd, and I know who he's looking for, because I've been trying to spot her too. When Alex finds his twin, his eyes deepen to a still calm. In seconds Rita is running toward him, tripping down the steps of the bleachers with my sister right behind her. The girls hug us both. I twist away from Molly's quick kiss, then shiver as Rita draws me to her and lets go too fast, almost before I have a chance to remember how it feels. Rita beams her famous smile right at me and says, loud and clear, "Thanks."

And now I'm dodging the fans streaming across the field, my body following my heart, headed straight for Uncle Gordo.

His arms are flung wide, his mouth still open in a shout—and next to him, stamping his feet and yelling just as loud, someone I never expected to see—my dad.

My father slaps my shoulder. "Hey, Dad," I say, and then I'm locked tight against my uncle, feeling his rough, crinkly jacket against my cheek.

My dad is watching us, puzzled; his head cocked to the side; he's obviously clueless. He doesn't realize how these twelve days in August have switched my life around, turned it so fast I feel like I've done a three-sixty in my uncle's Beemer.

"Great game!" Uncle Gordo yells. "Two assists!" He holds me at arm's length. "I saw what you did for number ten," he says.

"It wasn't just for Alex," I say, and then stop, too shy to go on. But Uncle Gordo must understand, because his glasses slide down his nose; he takes them off and wipes them on his sleeve.

"I know," he says. "I saw that, too."

Now my dad is really embarrassed, or nervous, or something—I can tell, because he's tugging his mustache like crazy. It feels good to be there with both of them, not caring what Dad thinks, turning instead to ask Uncle Gordo, "How's the Beemer?"

"Just fine," he says. "Still drives like a dream. Maybe when you're twenty-one, I'll give you another ride."

I laugh. And then Alex hurries past with the girls, moving light and easy the way he did his first day in Griswold. He's got his ball tucked under his arm. Rita gives us a shy wave and keeps going, but Alex stops, says to me, "Good game. Want a ride home? We've got the car for once."

I beckon to him. "Come meet my uncle. The one that gets me in trouble."

"Me!" Uncle Gordo protests. But he's laughing and shaking Alex's arm so hard I wonder if he might pump it off. "You play like an angel," Uncle Gordo says. "Really. And against the odds, I hear."

"It hasn't been easy," Alex admits. "But thanks. I love the game."

And Alex and my uncle give each other a look that reminds me a lot of twin e.s.p. I think maybe they understand each other in ways the rest of us will never know about. Or maybe I'm seeing things—maybe be-

*cause the lights are still making the grass shine a deep, summer green, because the stars, the noise of the crowd, and Rita's voice calling to me are all bumping each other inside my head—maybe that's why I hear and see things in a different way, on this warm night in August. Know what I mean?*

# Acknowledgments

Many friends helped with this book, including some who may not realize they were part of the journey. Thanks first of all to my sons, Derek and Ethan, who patiently answered my questions about soccer from their earliest days of playing the sport and continued to explain the intricacies of the game as I wrote the book.

During my years of watching from the sidelines, I was inspired by many young friends who played soccer with energy and enthusiasm. This is not their story, but I am particularly grateful to Caitlin Florschutz, Guen Gifford, Forrest Holzapfel, Scott Legere, Dylan Leiner, Catriona Rayl, Yuri Trump, and Jason and Damien Webster. Pete Davidson, an inspirational player who died soon after I started this book, taught me what it means to play the game—and the rest of your life—with all your heart.

I could not have finished this novel without the guidance and support of my writer's group: Eileen Christelow, Karen Hesse, and Bob MacLean. My thanks for their insightful criticism and unflagging humor as I shared draft after draft. Thanks also to my husband, Casey, and my friends Michael Fernandes, Michael Gigante, and Katherine Leiner, for the time they took to read the manuscript and share their reactions. I am also grateful to my editor, Margery Cuyler, to Kate and John Briggs at Holiday House, and to my agent, Gail Hochman, for their belief in my work.

Thanks to Avi, for reminding me, at a low point, how important it is to write the story we need to tell; to Kent Webster, who suggested it was time to create a boy's story; and to my students at Essex Middle School in Essex, Vermont, who kept me going with questions and comments about the novel's progress.

I regret that my friend and colleague, Betsey Bonin, will never know how much her commitment to books, children, and literacy meant to my work as a writer and teacher, especially as I wrote this novel. She created a community that built bridges between writers and readers of all ages. I will miss her very much.

Finally, I am deeply grateful to Michael Fernandes, whose open, loving friendship and passionate commitment to equality gave me the courage to write this story.